A MISHMOSH OF MURDER MYSTERY PLAYS

Volume 5

LEE MUELLER

Last Call At Chez Mort Copyright © 2011 by Lee Mueller

Death Near Dead Man's Holler Copyright © 2014 by Lee Mueller

A Murder Has Been Renounced Copyright © 2016 by Lee Mueller

All rights reserved.

No part of this book may be reproduced in any form or by any electronic or mechanical means, including information storage and retrieval systems, without written permission from the author, except for the use of brief quotations in a book review.

Caution: Professionals and amateurs are hereby advised that LAST CALL AT CHEZ MORT, DEATH NEAR DEAD MAN'S HOLLER, and A MURDER HAS BEEN RENOUNCED are subject to royalties. It is fully protected under the copyright laws.

CONTENTS

LAST CALL AT CHEZ MORT
A MURDER MYSTERY COMEDY PLAY

Characters	3
Act I	5
Act II	27

DEATH NEAR DEAD MAN'S HOLLER
A MURDER MYSTERY COMEDY PLAY

Characters	53
Act One	55
Act Two	93

A MURDER HAS BEEN RENOUNCED
COMEDY MURDER MYSTERY PLAY

Foreword	117
Preface	119
1. Act I	121
2. Act II	157
Afterword	187
Also by Lee Mueller	189

LAST CALL AT CHEZ MORT

A MURDER MYSTERY COMEDY PLAY

CHARACTERS

JEAN-PAUL TRUFFAUT- ("Juhn Paul True-foe") Host and Nightclub manager. A Frenchman with a thick accent. Is sometimes slow to understand what is happening around him. (can be played by female)

MACK - Streetwise Stage Manager. Typical 1940's hard boiled no nonsense guy.

LADY LELU- (lay-lou) Glamorous Night club singer. Has a bit of a hard shell under her beauty.

"BIG SUIT" STU - Sharped Dressed Gangster. Bark much worse than bite.

BODYGUARD- Stu's bodyguard. Speaks with Russian / German Accent. Not necessarily menacing in stature. A man (or woman) of few words and some of them English.

SWEET SUE- Ditsy Girlfriend of Big Suit Stu. Dreams of being as glamorous and popular as Lady LeLu. Unfortunately has no talent.

CHIEF INSPECTOR CONSTANTINE - Police inspector who has been around the block a few times. Slightly un-kept and shabby. Sometimes has an issue keeping his facts and names straight. He has worked so many cases they all are starting to run together.

SMITTY: News reporter.

Last Call At Chez Mort was originally produced and staged March 2011 by Affton Centerstage at Crestwood Art Space.

ACT 1

Setting is a night club. Original production set contained a small platform to serve as the bandstand (upstage) with an old fashion microphone. Stage left of the bandstand was a piano. Stage right of bandstand is a small table with a water pitcher and glasses. Downstage, are two cafe-style tables with chairs. On the walls behind the bandstand were old 1930's & 40's Jazz posters and various European club posters e.g. Folies Begere and La Chat Noir.

Time is the 40's. Pre-show Music should reflect this with Jazz of the era and Big band.

As the Play starts CONSTANTINE in a wrinkled overcoat enters followed by SMITTY. SMITTY wears a hat with a "PRESS" card stuck in the hatband. They look around for a moment.

CONSTANTINE: Ah yes! Club Chez Mort. What a swell place this was! A touch of European *joie de vivre* here in the heart of our city. Time it was and what a time it was. The memories.. the music, the dancing, the food. The ambiance. A bit of it still lingers, doesn't it Smitty?

SMITTY: Yea. There's some lingerin' goin' on.

CONSTANTINE: Such a nasty piece of business crumbled the whole cookie. You know, it's a shame a bad apple can ruin such a fruitful time.

SMITTY: Yea. It's a shame Inspector. It was a swell joint. Everybody's goin' over to that *La Chien Noir*[1] place now. Still, I hate to see it all end like this. On such a bad note.

CONSTANTINE: Very bad note. A most peculiar case this was! Most peculiar indeed. I can remember it as if... it were yesterday.

SMITTY: It *was* yesterday.

CONSTANTINE: Hmm? Was it? Oh yeah.

SMITTY: But don't let me stop you there inspector. I know you sometimes need to reminisce about these cases. Plus, it provides exposition.

CONSTANTINE: It what?

SMITTY: Exposition. For the paper. (*takes out notepad and pencil*) They promised me front page. I got most of the scoop, I just need to fill in a few details.

CONSTANTINE: Oh yeah, the details! (*takes a moment clears his throat*) From what I remember, it was a typical night here at Chez Mort. A night like any other.

Jazz Music fades up under CONSTANTINE's dialogue.

CONSTANTINE: (cont.) Folks dressed up to the nines. Stepping out in their Sunday best. They had completed a swell dinner. I believe prime rib and lobster Thermidor were on tap. Oh and the creme brûlée! What a tasty confection that is!

SMITTY: Isn't it though?

CONSTANTINE: Yes, so anyway, I believe the evening's entertainment was about to begin. Starting with some slight issues.

SMITTY: Slight issues huh?

CONSTANTINE: Yea. I believe the conflict began right away. Mr. Truffaut, the master of ceremonies had entered the room, to announce the entertainment..

Jean-Paul Truffaut, will appear as the music fades, he steps to the microphone. CONSTANTINE and SMITTY will silently exit.(note this is a flashback - perhaps a slight lighting change will help convey the change - such as bringing lights up full)

JEAN-PAUL: Bon soir and bonjour ladies and gentlemen, Mesdames and Messieurs. I hope you are enjoying ze time here at Club Chez Mort. Allow moi...me to introduce myself, I am ze host, your master of ceremony, Jean-Paul Truffaut. How about a nice applause for the musicians, yes? Merci! Yes, zey are très popular! But how can I speak about 'popular' and ze jazz milieu without mention of ze magnifique voice of ze lovely and talented voice of which I am certain you are here to see. So, without further adieu, may I bring to ze stage..

MACK quickly runs out to interrupt Jean-Paul. MACK is a stagehand he carries a clipboard.

MACK: Hey uh... Jean! Pal!

JEAN-PAUL: ..(cont..)..our premier singing sensation..

MACK: Yo Troofie!

Jean-Paul stops, somewhat embarrassed by the interruption. MACK quickly comes up to stage.

MACK: Excuse me, folks. We got a little technical matter here.. have some more hooch and nosh.

JEAN-PAUL: What is ze matter with ze technical?

MACK: (*testing microphone*) One.. two.. check. Yea, we're a little bright on the top. Bring 'er down a skosh.

MACK pulls JEAN-PAUL aside - as if out of earshot of the crowd.

JEAN-PAUL: What are you doing? I am in the middle of ze singing sensations...

MACK: What are *you* doing?

JEAN-PAUL: I am telling you what I am doing! Why do you ask what I am doing? I am asking you, what *you are* doing?

MACK: NO. I mean, what are you *doing*?

JEAN-PAUL: (*confused*) I am telling you. S'il vous plait! Why do you keep asking..

MACK: I mean, what are you doin' *introducing her*? Don't you remember *"who"* is supposed to be here tonight?

JEAN-PAUL: Here? Tonight? (*thinks and says the name of someone in audience*)

MACK: No, John Pauley! (*sighs*) Look! (*pulls farther aside*) Wise up Frenchie! Don't you remember the other day, when those 'mugs' came around here and gave us the business?

JEAN-PAUL: Gave us business? (*thinks*) Oh! You mean ze vending machine? Zey are wanting to refer ze business..

MACK: No, not *that* kinda business! I mean, the kind that's not on the up and up.

JEAN-PAUL: Not up up?

MACK: Yeah, not "up up". I'm talking about nasty business!

JEAN-PAUL: Ze nasty business? Monsieur Mack! Zis is a respectable club, we will have none of nasty..

MACK: No! I mean, *bad* business! Don't 'cha remember? Stu's crew!

JEAN-PAUL: Who crew? "Stu"?

MACK: Yea, Stu's crew. You know, those mugs that were in here the other day, swaggerin' around and smellin' up the joint!

JEAN-PAUL: Ah! Oui! Yes! Smelly swagger!

MACK: Right! 'Big Suit' Stu! The *meanest mug* in the city. Why there's talk that he's worse than 'Big-Eared' Lou!

JEAN-PAUL: Big ear who?

MACK: Big-Eared *Lou*. Leader of the Green Gang.

JEAN-PAUL: Gang? Green?

MACK: That's right Frenchie! But I ain't talkin about Big-Eared Lou, I'm talkin' about Big Suit Stu.

JEAN-PAUL: Not Lou, but Stu?

MACK: Right! See, Stu's the head of the East Side Mob. Big time goons. Nuthin' but trouble. Just like Big-Eared Lou.

JEAN-PAUL: Lou and Stu too?

MACK: Posi-lutely! But Stu is far more trouble!

JEAN-PAUL: Stu more than Lou?

MACK: You said it, brother!

JEAN-PAUL: Oui, I said something, but I don't know what! I am thinking you are not saying anything! I am interrupted for ze introduction by you to ask what I am doing! Pour quoi? To talk about Stu and Lou?

MACK: Simmer your teeth there Frenchie. What I'm tryin' to tell ya is that Stu don't want no dame singin' in this joint..

JEAN-PAUL: (*interrupts*) No singing?!

MACK: Right! Not unless it's his "Sweet Sue" doin' the tune.

JEAN-PAUL: Whose?

MACK: Stu's.

JEAN-PAUL: Stu's?

MACK: Yea, Stu!

JEAN-PAUL: Stu wants to sing?

MACK: No, not Stu! Sue!

JEAN-PAUL: Who?

MACK: Sue! Stu wants Sweet Sue to sing.

JEAN-PAUL: Who is Sue?

MACK: That broad that's been hangin' around the band. Ya see, Sue belongs to Stu.

JEAN-PAUL: Je ne sais pas. (*takes out handkerchief -wipes brow*) But.. but.. I do not follow zis Lou, Stu.. Sue sing?

MACK: Look Frenchie, all I'm tryin to tell ya, if you bring Lady Lelu out here to sing and Stu walks in here... well, brother, there's gunna be trouble!

JEAN-PAUL: Stu's brother will be in trouble?

MACK: No, *you'll* be in trouble.

JEAN-PAUL: *I'll* be?

MACK: And how!

JEAN-PAUL: And how.. will I be?

MACK: Up to your eyeballs pal!

JEAN-PAUL: My eyeballs?!

MACK: Right! Look, If I was you, I'd switch up things tonight. Just till it blows over.

JEAN-PAUL: But see... zere is.. how do you say, a 'wee' problem.

MACK: A wee problem.

JEAN-PAUL: Quoi?

MACK: "A *Wee problem*". That's how I say it. Just like that.

JEAN-PAUL: Yes! (*beat*) No, no! I am saying.. ze wee problem is.. many of zese fine people who are here...(*nervously surveys audience*) are here to...zey have come for.. to see ze lovely Siren of the City. The Lady Lelu! And you are to telling me, zat she is not to sing? But zey are here to see her sing?

MACK: I know what they're here for.. but Big Suit Stu is gunna be here to see Sue sing! If you insist on the Lelu broad instead.. well, how do you say "mincemeat"?

JEAN-PAUL: I do not say mincemeat!

MACK: Well ya better learn how to say it, because you'll *be* it.

JEAN-PAUL: (*nervous*) Oh... what do I do?

MACK: Let me spell it out for ya pal; if ya go with Sue, you get no Stu. If ya go with Lelu, I'd hate to be you.

JEAN-PAUL: But..but..

LADY *LELU enters*

LADY LELU: Hey you big lugs! What's going on out here? Are you going to introduce me or what?

LELU tries to take bandstand but JEAN-PAUL attempts to block her way.

JEAN-PAUL: Oh! Lady Lelu! Zere is something..I cannot.. I uh...

LADY LELU: What's he yammering about?

MACK: He's got a "wee problem".

LADY LELU: A *wee problem*? Has he tried cranberry juice?

MACK: No, that's not what he.. tell her Truffie.

LADY LELU: Tell me what?

JEAN-PAUL: Ummmm.. yes. How do you say, much trouble...

LADY LELU: "Much trouble". I say it just like that.

JEAN-PAUL: Yes! No, no! I mean, much trouble with ze Stu.

LADY LELU: Trouble with the Stu? Try adding more salt!

MACK: Naw he's talking about *Big Suit* Stu.

LADY LELU: That two-bit hood? What about him?

JEAN-PAUL: Oui. He is having Mincemeat!

LELU: Look, I don't care what he wants to order. I'm a singer, not a waitress. You got me Pops? Now step aside and let's get this show on the road! My fans are waitin'. (*pushing Jean-Paul aside*) Come on boys!

JEAN-PAUL: But wait! No..

LELU: Look Jean-Paul, I ain't waitin' around for ya to solve your wee problem.

JEAN-PAUL: But the Stu..

LELU: I told ya, add some salt! I ain't got time.

MACK: Well, we tried Frenchie, come on.

LAST CALL AT CHEZ MORT

MACK leads JEAN-PAUL off - Jean-Paul mumbles and weeps as they exit.

Music will start (Note: originally we had piano player but this can be pre-recorded music -e.g. Karaoke version or lip-sync) LELU sing a song of the time period -originally song was "Someone To Watch Over Me" by Gershwin.

When the song concludes JEAN-PAUL will come quickly back on stage as if to stop LADY LELU from doing another song.

LADY LELU: Thank you ladies and gentlemen. It's so nice to be here at Club Chez Mort. For my next number, I would like to..

JEAN-PAUL: Very well, thank you Merci. Zat has been enough for now. (*steps up on platform bumping Lelu off*)

LELU: What? Enough?

JEAN-PAUL: Oui. It is... (*thinks*) Ze sound! Yes! It is technical matter. Bad with sound.

LELU: Technical matter? It sounded fine!

JEAN-PAUL: Yes! No, no! I believe it is.. how you say, ze microphone.

LELU: "The Microphone". I say it like that!

JEAN-PAUL: Oui! No, no! Ze microphone. It is.. out of tune!

LELU: Out of tune?

JEAN-PAUL: Oui! (*takes out pencil and taps the microphone, holds pencil up to his ear*) Yes! The tune is sharp! Monsieur Mack! Come and fix zis, yes?

LELU: You're talkin' like ya fell on your head!

Through the audience should enter BIG SUIT STU. A bodyguard will hover behind him -STU's suit should be a few sizes too large - perhaps extra padding in shoulders.

STU: I'll say somebody fell on their head!

LELU: Yea? Well, you're a little late there pal. I already said that!

STU: (*chuckles*) She already said that! Did you hear that? Funny! What's also funny is I thought we had an understanding. Yea. See, I believe I requested a certain doll to sing in this dump tonight. And.. (*looks around*) I don't see her. That could be a problem because I had it on good authority Sue was singin' in this dive tonight!

LADY LELU: Who?

STU: Sue!

LADY LELU: Sue? (*to Jean-Paul*) Who's that?

JEAN-PAUL: Stu!

LADY LELU: Stu?

STU: (*pointing at LELU*) Who's she?

LADY LELU: (*to STU*) Lady Lelu that's who! Who are you supposed to be?

STU: I'm *supposed to be* here to hear my Sweet Sue sing.

LADY LELU: Sweet Sue? You mean Sue Blutowsky? (*laughs*) Are you kiddin' me? Why that yodeler can't even carry a tune in a bucket!

JEAN-PAUL: Yes! No, no! He is making ze mincemeat.

LADY LELU: Again with the mincemeat! The kitchen's back that way Pal. Chop chop!

STU: Kitchen? Pardon me toots, but I don't like your attitude.

LADY LELU: And I don't like your suit. Did your mother dress you?

STU *snaps his fingers and bodyguard comes forward.*

STU: What if she did? You wanna make something of it?

LADY LELU: Not sure I could make anything out it. Maybe a nice rag rug or pillow stuffin'.

STU: Wait! Did you say rag stuffin'?

    SWEET SUE runs out on stage as if late, which breaks the tension. She is barefoot.

SUE: Woo-hoo! Here I am Stu sweetie! I was just gettin' changed and warmin' up my pipes. *(She sings a short off-key scale - also pours water into glass from the pitcher and loudly gargles)*

LADY LELU: What's that noise?! Sounds like someone strangling a Pekingese!

JEAN-PAUL: *(nervous)* à quoi bon!? I must go and see to uh.. something. *(starts to exit)*

STU: Wait a second!

    STU snaps his fingers and BODYGUARD, approaches JEAN-PAUL

STU: *(continues)* My friend, Mr. Raskolnikov[2] is willing to assist you. Perhaps, he can help you straighten out this little matter.

JEAN-PAUL: What? Oh! Is nothing ze matter. It is fine. Miss Sue, s'il vous plaît! Please. If you wish to entertain..

LELU: Hey! What's the big idea? You're going let that two-bit crook snap your cap?

STU: Why don't you take a powder Lelu.

LELU: Aw says you! Why don't you mind your potatoes and dry up!

STU: Keep talkin' why don't cha!

LELU: Oh yea? What are you going to do ya big lug? Fill us full of daylight? In front of all these people?

JEAN-PAUL: Please, Miss Lelu!

LELU: Aw! He's just a wet sock, Truffaut.

JEAN-PAUL: I know but..!

LELU: Oh swell! Crumble like a cookie why don't you? Fine! If you wanna let this palooka turn you into a wet blanket, Fine! La Chien Noir has been after me to sing there. Maybe I'll take 'em up on the offer. At least that dive has class. (*she storms off*)

STU: You know, that broad's not bad. A real tomato! She's gotta lotta moxie.

SUE: What about me?

STU: You? You got spunk, baby. Not so much on the moxie.

SUE: No! I mean, do I get ta sing now or what?

STU: Oh that. Yea Johnny. You heard the lady. Does she get ta sing or what?

JEAN-PAUL: It's Jean (*juhn*) Is not Johnny!

STU: Wait! It's what?

JEAN-PAUL: Uhh.. it is fine.

STU: I think he hears pretty well, but his brain don't work so good. (*to Bodyguard*) Maybe you can give him a good idea.

BODYGUARD: Da! (*Russian Accent*) We are wanting Sue to sing. (*he reaches under coat and brings out a small Hatchet*)

STU: Meet my associate. Don't give him no trouble neither. He's been havin' problems with his landlady. He's a bit touchy.

JEAN-PAUL: (*seeing hatchet*) Oui! Of course! Yes. Please! Sue can sing. Please! Yes!

LAST CALL AT CHEZ MORT

BODYGUARD: Spasiba. (*spa-see-bah*) -(*he puts hatchet back in coat*)

JEAN-PAUL: Excusez-moi! I must go... (*starts to exit*)

BODYGUARD: I come with you, no?

JEAN-PAUL: No! I mean, oui. Yes. If you must. (*quickly exits*)

    BODYGUARD *follows JEAN-PAUL off at a slower menacing pace - perhaps making eye contact with members of audience - saying "What are you looking at?! etc.."*

SUE: Stu baby? Can I sing now?

STU: Of course doll face.. wait! Where's your shoes?

SUE: What? (*looks down*) Oh! Ha! I couldn't find them!

STU: Couldn't find them?

SUE: No. I took 'em off somewhere for some reason and...

STU: Well never mind that. Go ahead and serenade us with a sweet song.

SUE: Swell! You're the cat's pajamas Stu!

STU: Thanks. (*beat*) Wait! What? Was that a crack about my suit?

SUE: Of course not Stu face. I'm just sayin' you're the most!

STU: Oh thanks. (*beat*) Wait! I'm the *most* what?

SUE: Oh you big silly crumb! Sit down will ya!

STU: OK, sure! Anything for you doll.

    STU sits at table. SUE should warm up again briefly.

SUE: Gee willa-kers folks. Ain't this a kick! This is my first time in front of a crowd. I wanna thank Johnny Paul and everyone here at the Club Chez (*she will pronounce it CHEESE*) Mort for givin' me this swell opportunity! But most of all, I wanna thank my little Stu bear for arranging things for me. Nobody ever thought I had any talent, except him. He's just aces! I'd like to dedicate this to Stu. All right. I'm ready when you are. In the key of E sharp. Let's hit it!

She will begin singing and it should be somewhat painful to hear.

She will sing the classic "Let's Call The Whole Thing Off" -however her reading on the lyrics should be wrong: for the opening verse -"You Say Potato, I say Potato" she will pronounce both the same.

For the sake of all concerned, only let her sing for a short time NOTE: Sue should not touch the Microphone stand until her demise is determined. What should happen is she reaches out and grabs the Microphone stand - Immediately a look of SHOCK should occur as she halts singing - It should appear as if she is being electrocuted as she holds the stand - perhaps she convulses in place and makes fluttering vocal noise. Maybe the lights dim and a strobe effect.

She does this for a moment or two and then drops down dead to floor. Music stops.

BIG SUIT STU will cross up to SUE.

STU: Sweet Sue! Sweet Sue! What happened?! (*bends down to check her*) Sue? Speak to me doll!

Stu *lifts her wrist to check her pulse -bows his head for a moment, lets her limp arm fall back to floor. He stands back up.*

STU: (*calling out*) All right! That tears it! (*looks around room -especially audience members sitting close to stage area. If possible, he pulls out gun from inside suit and waves it around*) Which one of you mugs done her in? Was it *you*? (*indicates someone in audience*) Who put the kabosh on my Sweet Sue?! How bout you? (*picks another member of audience*)

MACK comes out and walks toward stage

MACK: What's all the hub-bub?

STU: Wait! What? What did you call me?

MACK: I didn't call you nothin' pal. And why don't you stop waving that lead dispencer around. You could put someone's eye out. Hey Band! A little help here!

Music plays begins softly under - e.g. Moonlight Serenade - Glenn Miller

STU: Wait! What did you... what's your name pal?

MACK: The name's McElroy but you can call me... Gertrude. (*looks at Sue*) What happened to the dame?

    Bodyguard *rushes out*

BODYGUARD: What ease it boss?

STU: What do ya mean, '*what ease it?*' What's it look like? Huh?! Look! It's Sue! She was singin' and now.. she's *not*!

MACK: It looks like Sue's taking the big sleep.

BODYGUARD: Why does she sleep?

STU: She's not asleep you sap, she's... she's..

MACK: Dead.

BODYGUARD: Why she dead?

STU: How do I know!? I'm not a rocket surgeon! All I know is she was fine till.. she touched that! (*looking at microphone stand*)

BODYGUARD: What? She touch that and go to big sleep die?

STU: Yea pal. Big sleep die. There's somethin' rotten here, I tell ya. And it ain't just the food. I'm bettin; somebody had it in for her! (*walks around stage area -looks at glass and water pitcher*) I'll bet she was *poisoned..(turns pointing to microphone)* by *that* thing!

MACK: How's that again?

STU: You heard me! I didn't stutter pal.

MACK: Maybe not, but it sounded like you said she was poisoned by the microphone?

BODYGUARD: (*looking at Microphone*) Is too much juice!

STU: What'd'ya mean juice?! She ain't drunk! She's dead!

MACK: What you're comrade is sayin' is - maybe there was a short in the wiring and she became ground.

STU: I can see she's on the *ground*! I want to know why?!

MACK: Listen, Einstein, we're talking about the microphone! When she touched it, it lit her up like a Christmas tree.

BODYGUARD: Da! Sue shocked to big sleep!

STU: Wait! What are you saying Gertrude? Are you saying Sweet Sue was shocked while she sang?

MACK: Yea! Sweet sue was shocked while she sang. And now she's selling seashells by the seashore.

STU: Wait! She's what?

BODYGUARD: She need doctor.

MACK: She's beyond a doctor. She needs a step ladder to start picking turnips.

STU: (*points gun at Mack*) Why you I oughta..!!!

MACK: There's plenty of time for that later, but don't you think we call the local peeper about the stiff dame?

STU: Wait! Call the what?

MACK: The flatfoots, the gumshoes. Maybe this was an accident and maybe it wasn't.

STU: Oh No! No coppers!

JEAN-PAUL rushes out

JEAN-PAUL: Sacré bleu! What has going to happened?

STU: I'll tell you *what has going to happen*! Trouble! That's what'll happen! If I don't find out what...happened here!

JEAN-PAUL: What does he saying? What is happen?

MACK: What's happened is Suzy here got jolted like Sacco and Vanzetti in the hot seat. And now, Stu thinks somebody gummed up the works.

STU: You! (*points at Jean-Paul*) You didn't want my Sweet Sue to sing! I bet it was you! You gummed it up pal!

JEAN-PAUL: Moi? But.. I do not have gum!

STU: And why not? I like gum! It's refreshing! Maybe I should take you for a little ride and buy you a stick! And maybe you can tell me what you did to my Sweet Sue!

MACK: Don't be a sap Stu. Frenchie wouldn't hurt a fly. Unless it was doin' the backstroke in someone's soup. Stop being such a hard-boiled and use your Stu sized brain. Maybe it was faulty wiring, did you ever think of that?

JEAN-PAUL: No! Ze wiring is *not* faulty. Zere is nothing faulty here at Chez Mort! No, no, no!

MACK: *Ick-snay* on the *aulty-fay* Frenchie, I'm trying to save your skin. Ya know? Remember? Mincemeat?

JEAN-PAUL: Oh! Yes, oui, oui oui! Tres bein. You know, oui! Perhaps zere is a.. how you say? Ze "faulty" wire.. technical matter. Yes. Of course! Faulty, faulty!

STU: The only thing faulty around here is *you guys*. I'm having a real problem with your stories.

MACK: Yea well, the real problem I'm havin' is with this story! (*indicates Sue*) How bout the story on what do we do?

JEAN-PAUL: What we do?

MACK: Yea, Stu got the heebie-jeebies when I mentioned calling the officials to sort this mess out.

JEAN-PAUL: Oui! We should call ze laws! Tout suite! Yes!

STU: I said, "No Cops"! (*points gun*)

JEAN-PAUL: Yes! No, no! Of course! No cops! No, no!

MACK: Aw that's swell! So what do we do, Stu? Stand around beating our gums till your doll turns ripe?

STU: I've have enough of your yap Gertrude!

MACK: Oh yea? So what do you wanna do Stu?

JEAN-PAUL: Yes! We do something! (*turns to audience*) Forgive me ladies and gentlemen. Je suis désolé! I am sorry for zis event. We must continue with ze evening programs! (*turns to STU*) We must remove this Sue and.. ce qu'il est, how do say?

MACK: The show must go on?

JEAN-PAUL: Oui!

STU: "We" ain't doin' a thing! Not until I say so.

MACK: Yea, that's just swell! Let's just leave a dead body right here. Right at your feet. In front of all these witnesses.

STU: (*looks around*) Ok wait! Maybe we should... you know. Tidy things up a bit.

    STU *snaps his fingers and the Bodyguard comes to him. Stu whispers to him, pointing to Sue's body and then points elsewhere.*

MACK, STU *and Bodyguard lift* SUE *and carry her off.* JEAN PAul *nervously follows trying to help.*

SMITTY *and Constantine will walk out amongst the action -watching* SUE *getting carried off. They are not Acknowledged by cast.*

CONSTANTINE: (*enters*) Well, Smitty, after receiving a frantic, albeit *anonymous* telephone call from a concerned patron, I arrived here at Club Chez Mort about this time.

JEAN-PAUL enters and comes to the microphone as if to speak. Almost touches it but jumps back.

JEAN-PAUL: Yes, a thank you to the patience.. as you have known, a most terrible.. occurrence has.. occurred. An accident has happened and..

JEAN-PAUL: ..I do not wish you to spoil your delight in our evening because of this. We will see to you...

CONSTANTINE: Ah yes! This, I believe is where I came in.

INSPECTOR CONSTANTINE enters stage area.

CONSTANTINE: Right! Here now, what's all this then?

JEAN-PAUL: Oh, oui, Ladies and gentlemen, yes, it is.. It is.. how do you say..?

CONSTANTINE: Inspector Eddie Constantine, is how I say it. Special investigations. It's my duty to inform you, a woman *may* have met her end in may I say.. a deliberate fashion. She was in the midst of singing when..

JEAN-PAUL: Uh..pardon Inspector but.. zey (*indicates audience*) were here. Zey have seeing it with eyes.

CONSTANTINE: Right! As I suspected. (*pulls out notepad*) The unfortunate demise of the entertainer, a one.. Sour Sally..

JEAN-PAUL: Pardon moi, is Sweet Sue.

CONSTANTINE: Right! Sweet Sue... Sure! Of course! From my brief preliminary investigation, it appears a particular "malfunction" was initiated to the amplification device in which she conducted her entertainment. A connection may have been manipulated in such a way, as to produce a raw electric current to propagate through her being thus causing her demise.

JEAN-PAUL: Uh.. I am sorry? Is zis English you speak?

MACK enters

MACK: He's saying that some mug may have fiddled with the wiring. And when Sweet Sue touched the mic stand, she got the juice and a one way ticket to the great gig in the sky.

CONSTANTINE: (*to Mack*) And I'm sorry, but is that English you speak?

MACK: Good question pal, but I think the question should be, who jimmied the wires?

CONSTANTINE: "Jimmied"?

JEAN-PAUL: Jimmy? I do not know Jimmy.

MACK: Right. There's only one way a mic would short out like that. And that's if someone mickied with the grounding wire.

JEAN-PAUL: I do not know Mickey.

CONSTANTINE: Exactly! On what grounds? But first, we must ask, where would Jimmy or Mickey pull this wire?

MACK: We ain't go no "Jimmy" here pops! But there should be a grounding wire terminated on the breaker box in the back.

CONSTANTINE: I see. I will have to check into that. But now, if we are to assume it was deliberate, a wire was exploited, then we must ask, who was near this breaker box?

JEAN-PAUL: It was Jimmy?

CONSTANTINE: Well, bring Jimmy out here and let's question him!

MACK: Look pal, it's a figure of speech. Like I said,

there ain't no Jimmy here.

CONSTANTINE: Of course not! Jimmy is probably long gone by now. And probably took Micky with him.

JEAN-PAUL: Why would he put the wire from the ground?

CONSTANTINE: Why indeed!

MACK: Indeed inspector, but here the thing-- there was nuthin wrong with it earlier. That's what I don't get.

CONSTANTINE: How's that?

MACK: Earlier tonight, when Frenchie and I was out here. I checked the mic. It was fine.

CONSTANTINE: Fine you say?

MACK: Fine I say.

CONSTANTINE: Well that's fine! That fact would remove any doubt of circumstance and point to deliberate intent! I'll need to take a look around. If you could show me these areas?

MACK: No problem. This way pal! (*Mack exits*)

JEAN-PAUL will pace around bandstand muttering to himself. CONSTANTINE walks downstage.

CONSTANTINE: And so Smitty, I sussed out the situation.

SMITTY: So that's the story so far?

CONSTANTINE: Yep. To this point. Best I can recall.

SMITTY: (*refers to notepad*) That's pretty much the scoop I got as well. Except for Stu's bodyguard. I got it different. Yea, word he was a *German* fella, named Hans Beckert. Not a Russian, like in your story.

CONSTANTINE: German? Was he now? I seem to remember a Russian in some story. Perhaps something I was reading. A crime that I don't recall. I guess that's my punishment!

SMITTY: So, what happened next?

CONSTANTINE: Next, I went off looking for clues and whatnot. I believe they had a brief respite in the meantime.

SMITTY: A brief..what?

CONSTANTINE: An interim. In the evening's activities. As I am to understand, an entr'acte was announced.

SMITTY: A what?

JEAN-PAUL goes up and speaks into Microphone.

JEAN-PAUL: Bonjour ladies and gentlemen, Mesdames and Messieurs once again. I do apologize for ze unfortunate event. Please, we shall take a short rest for ze time here.

SMITTY: Oh an intermission!

CONSTANTINE and SMITTY exit.

JEAN-PAUL. If you please, take a few moments and... we will continue at some time soon.. later... merci.

JEAN-PAUL bows and exits.

-END OF ACT I

---

1. La Sh-yen N-war
2. Raz-coal-na-cough

ACT II

❧

JEAN-PAUL enters and speaks into Microphone.

JEAN-PAUL: Bonjour ladies and gentlemen, again I am to say for ze ..uh I am to apologize. Never before has something like zis to happen. It is most calm here at Chez Mort now yes? No more interruptions shall be or problems, no, no!

MACK and CONSTANTINE enter speaking silently to each other.

JEAN-PAUL: (*cont.*) We will have no more of the nasty business that is not .. up up. Very nice now yes? Most how you say.. pleasant? We are calm and peaceful now, yes?

LADY LELU comes out followed by Stu

LELU: Get your mitts off me! What are your intentions?!

STU: Well, fine! Be like that! At least tell me why babe?!

LELU: Will somebody tell this big Lug to beat it!

STU: But Loo loo baby..

ACT II

LELU: I ain't your baby. And if you try to touch me with your filthy paws one more time, why I'll...!

MACK: What gives toots?

LELU: I'll tell ya what gives! This big palooka! He gives me a headache!

MACK: Why don't you leave the doll alone Stu.

STU: Oh yea? Says who?

MACK: Says me.

STU: Oh yea?

MACK: Yea.

STU: What are you? Some kinda wise guy?

JEAN-PAUL: Pardonne moi, Mr. Big Stu, you have met ze uh... Inspector Constantine, yes?

STU: Expect a constant what?

CONSTANTINE: Inspector Eddie Constantine. Special investigations, crime division.

STU: If that don't beat all! I said no cops!

CONSTANTINE: Did you, Pal? You said, "no cops?" And why is that?

STU: Well, it would.. uh... because you see... tell him Hanzy!

Bodyguard *will now speak with a German accent*

BODYGUARD: Vat is dis mein Stu?

CONSTANTINE: Hanzy? Would that happen to be a variation of Hans? As in Hans Beckert? Or should I say, Hans the Hatchet? The notorious Russian!

MACK: *German.*

ACT II

CONSTANTINE: I mean, German.

BODYGUARD: Wie bitte? Nine the hatchet!

CONSTANTINE: Nine? I thought you carried only one. I had no idea.

STU: Say, what's the big idea anyway?

MACK: I dunno Stu. Maybe the good inspector has an idea?

CONSTANTINE: Hang on! Did you say "Stu"?

MACK: I believe, perhaps I did utter somethin' like that. Maybe I should say, "Big Suit Stu".

CONSTANTINE: Well, well, well. *Big Suit Stu!* of the East Side Mob. And *Heini the Hatchet,* just my luck! Both of you, here on this evening. And might I add, most interesting that a young lady should turn up mortified with you two around.

STU: I had nothing to do with any mortification! You can't pin this on me, see? I was here to see Sue! Sue was my sweetie. She was singing for me and me only.

LELU: I'm not sure I would call what she was doing "singing".

CONSTANTINE: And you my dear, are Lady Lavender, aren't you?

LELU: It's Lady Lelu.

CONSTANTINE: Of course it is. You are the featured entertainer here right?

LELU: Wrong! More like "w*as*".

CONSTANTINE: Was? And why's that?

LELU: You tell me! I get to do *one* number and the next thing I know, Frenchie's out here yammerin about some technical thing and I get pulled for Sue Bluwtosky. The singin' banshee.

ACT II

STU: Hey! Watch it you!

LELU: Ah! So's your old man!

CONSTANTINE: Technical thing? I see! So, just prior to Miss Suzie Blue Banshee taking the stage, you were out here in the very same space with the very same equipment. This microphone, is that correct?

LELU: Yea, that's correct.

CONSTANTINE: Did you, in fact, touch it?

LADY LELU: In fact, I may have.

CONSTANTINE: And from what we may surmise, Miss Laven..uh Lu..Lola, you're still living and breathing?

LELU: Lelu! I dunno, let me check. (*she feels her own pulse*) Well, what do you know? The clock's still tickin'! Imagine that, will ya?

CONSTANTINE: Yes, I will imagine that. I'll also imagine as this gentleman stated (*indicates MACK*) the microphone was "fine" when he checked it earlier. And it was fine during your song. So, this sudden electrical mishap, happened after you sang.

LELU: You figured that out all by yourself?

CONSTANTINE: Yep! I will also need to figure who was present when Miss Sunny Sweetly..

MACK: Sweet Sue..

CONSTANTINE: .. when "Sweet Sue" was on stage. I take it that all of you were present in this region?

JEAN-PAUL: How you say, all were here to present in regions.

CONSTANTINE: Is that right? Every last one of you?

ACT II

STU: Oh no! Not every last one! All of us were not.. all to present! *They* were not present in the regions! I didn't see them regionally.. here!

CONSTANTINE: I almost understood that, but if you please, who are you referring to Stu?

STU: I'm referring to that French mug and the wise guy. And that other broad.

CONSTANTINE: By *French guy* you mean Mr. Truffaut. And by wise guy you mean... ?

STU: Gertrude!

CONSTANTINE: Gertrude?

JEAN-PAUL: Who is ze Gertrude?

MACK: He means me.

CONSTANTINE: Ah! OK! Gertrude.

MACK: Actually Inspector, the name's Mack.

CONSTANTINE: Mack? Very good, Mack! (*beat*) So, Gertrude, you and Mr. Truffaut and Lady Lola were not around while Sweet Sally was singing?

MACK: Yea, that's right. See, I run the works behind the scenes. Making sure everyone's where they're supposed to be. I ain't paid to be out here lollygagging around and bumpin gums.

CONSTANTINE: Got it Gertrude. And the Frenchman?

JEAN-PAUL: Moi? But I was.. seeing to Lady Lelu. She was most upset by ze problems. Madame was saying she is going to leave, to work for ze *Chien Noir* Club. I cannot let her do zis! I go to see for her.

CONSTANTINE: Upset by the *problems*?

ACT II

JEAN-PAUL: Yes! Of course! But zis Stu was not to want Lady Lelu to sing. No, no! He was preferred the Sweet Sue.

CONSTANTINE: So, Stu preferred Sue over Lelu?

JEAN-PAUL: Oui, but see, pardon moi, but zis sweet Sue..she can't sing good.

STU: Says you!

CONSTANTINE: So, Stu wanted Sue to sing?

JEAN-PAUL: True.

CONSTANTINE: What's true?

JEAN-PAUL: True, Stu didn't want Lelu.

CONSTANTINE: I see. So, Stu upset Lelu. So Sue sang?

JEAN-PAUL: True Sue sings. Zat upsets Lelu! Lelu is to leave. She cannot. I went to see.

CONSTANTINE: Uh-huh. What about you, Stu?

STU: What about me? I was out here in plain sight. Ask anybody in the joint.

CONSTANTINE: (*to audience*) So you all saw Mr. Stu did you? (*wait for response*) Very well, who else was not present?

BODYGUARD: Gertrude!

MACK: I told ya, I run things backstage! I'm the *stage manager*.

STU: Is that right?

MACK: Yea, that's right.

STU: Well, you didn't *manage* to keep Sue safe on this stage, did ya now?

MACK: Listen pal, I *managed* to check that mic a million times. There was nuthin' wrong with it.

32

ACT II

STU: Wait! Nuthin wrong?! Did you say nuthin wrong?

MACK: That's what I said! Anything coulda happened. It coulda shorted out in the stand, in the box-- a dozen places. Who knows? I ain't an electrician.

STU: You ain't?

LELU: Shocking, ain't it?

STU: Yea, it sure is. Say, why don't you check it now Gertrude?

MACK: Check it?

STU: Yea. Check the microphone now! Let's see what happens.

JEAN-PAUL: No! Is faulty!

STU: Let's see how faulty!

CONSTANTINE: Gentlemen, I wouldn't advise..

LELU: Don't do it Mack!

MACK: Fine! I will.

MACK goes to stand and grabs it.

MACK: (*cont.*) There! Ya happy? Nuthin wrong with it.

LELU: (*to Stu*) Probably cause you fixed it!

STU: I didn't fix nuthin'.

LELU: Then why didn't he get shocked?

STU: Search me.

MACK: What doesn't shock me is what Stu failed to mention. He failed to tell ya that Hans the Hatchet was also backstage messin' around. How do we know he didn't do a lumberjack number on the wires? Huh?

STU: Oh yeah?

ACT II

MACK: Yeah! And then fixed it back all nice after Sue got grilled.

STU: Is that what you think?

MACK: I don't think, I know!

STU: Yeah, well, I don't think *you know*.

MACK: And I don't think you think!

STU: Oh you think so, do ya?

MACK: I think I already said that.

STU: You all ready... wait! What did you say?

MACK: Well, what do you know.

CONSTANTINE: Well, *I know*, the facts are that Mr. Truffaut, Lady Loo, Gertrude and Hans were not around at the time of the incident. This fact, provides opportunity for any one of them to fiddle with the wiring. Now, the question is.. who had motive?

STU: I'm laying odds on the Frenchmen! He didn't want my Sweet Sue stealing the spotlight from his precious Lelu!

LELU: Oh please Stu! The only thing your Sue could steal was the audience's dough. No one would pay to hear her screeching!

CONSTANTINE: But it would seem someone made her "pay" as it were. The question would be, who was here to collect?

LELU: Are you kiddin' me? This is Sue Blutosky we're talkin about! A half portion canary! Why she's had more guys than Carter's got pills.

STU: Why you!

ACT II

LELU: Go ahead ya slug faced goon! You were just the latest butter and egg man for that dizzy broad. Be thankful you don't have a heart otherwise she woulda walked all over it pal!

CONSTANTINE: Funny you should mention hearts, Miss Loolay, because that reminds me, I was just about to mention that I found something very interesting. A letter. (*takes out letter*)

JEAN-PAUL: A letter?

STU: A Letter?

LADY LELU: Letter?

CONSTANTINE: Yes. A letter. It looks like it was composed by the late Sweet singer to someone... unknown.

STU: Wait! Where did you get this letter?

CONSTANTINE: Not very long ago after making the rounds, I found a folded letter, laying backstage. The shock of its subject may have sparked the "shock" on the stage. A vital clue may lie within.

MACK: Well, what does it say?

CONSTANTINE: It doesn't *say* anything. One has to read it.

Allow me to read:

My dearest Lovey Dove, Spelled D.U.V, ..*Please don't be sore. It's not you, it's me. The only reason I am with Big Suit Stu is because he is tops in the city and he can get me to the top. He can help me be a swell singer and get me into the best joints in the city. That is the only reason. I know you've been a good Joe and tried to help. I still have feelings for you. I always will. Please don't be miffed. Your bestest doll, Sweet Sue.*

STU: That's it?

CONSTANTINE: That's all she wrote.

LELU: In more ways than one.

ACT II

MACK: Ain't it touchin'?

LELU: What did I tell ya? I told you.

MACK: So what are you thinkin' Inspector? This *lovey dove* got sore cause she played him for a sap? So, he snuck in here and lit her up like the Great White Way?

CONSTANTINE: It may be a possibility, as you so colorfully put it.

MACK: So who's Lovey Dove?

CONSTANTINE: There's the rub! Who indeed!

JEAN-PAUL: Maybe it is Jimmy?

MACK: There ain't no Jimmy!

JEAN-PAUL: But he is to ask?

MACK: If you ask me, who's to say Stu over here didn't get wind of this letter and find out she was givin' him the high hat? A trip for biscuits. So he sent one of his torpedos to tumble the whole game.

LELU: You said it brother! And how!

STU: That's enough out of you two! I oughta!

LELU: You oughta what? Take us for ride like you do everybody who double-crosses you? Like poor Sue did? Huh?

 STU *visibly upset snaps his fingers. Bodyguard crosses toward LADY LELU reaching in coat as if to get his Hatchet.*

CONSTANTINE: That's enough with the rough stuff!

 Bodyguard *stops and simply pulls out a handkerchief from his coat and blows his nose.*

ACT II

MACK: Remember who you're dealing with here Stu. Constantine is johnny law. One false move and it's straight to the hoosegow with you!

STU: Ah go on! Quit razzing me, Gertrude!

CONSTANTINE: I said, that's enough! Thank you. Now, let us proceed in a dignified manner. As I had stated, this letter indicates that Miss Sweet Cindy..

STU: Sue!

CONSTANTINE: Yes, Sweet Sue, had upset a certain party in her sudden association with Big-Eared Lou..

MACK: Big Suit Stu!

CONSTANTINE: ..Yes, yes, whatever! This letter states that she was looking to forward her career as a nightclub entertainer, et cetera et cetera and it steamed up someone in this room! Now, this raises the question, who?

SMITTY enters slightly -Cast freezes - they will not acknowledge him or exchange with CONSTANTINE.

SMITTY: Yea Inspector, who?! That does raise the question, doesn't it?

CONSTANTINE: I'm sorry?

SMITTY: I mean, sure I know the scoop, but still it makes you kinda wonder.

CONSTANTINE: Oh yes, I did wonder.

SMITTY: I'm sure ya did Eddie. I mean, look at these mugs! I mean, ya could pin it on any one of 'em. The gangster here coulda been fed up and had the Gerry cut the wire. Or it coulda been the French guy or the Lelu broad. I woulda run all of 'em in and grilled 'em under the hot lights till somebody fessed up.

ACT II

CONSTANTINE: Actually, that would be standard operating procedure, however, the logistics did not lend itself that luxury.

SMITTY: What?

CONSTANTINE: What I mean to say is, had this been an average evening or even a run of the mill place, that would be the case. But this case was not average. Since the crowd were witnesses to the alleged crime... I mean, our interrogation room couldn't handle them all. So, I took a less than average approach.

SMITTY: Is that right? What did you do?

CONSTANTINE: Something like this-- (*turns his attention back to stage area*) Now, since everyone here was privy to the events that unfolded, it may be beneficial to invite you, the Chez Mort patrons to question the parties involved.

SMITTY: So, let me get this straight. You actually let the crowd ask questions?

CONSTANTINE: Yes. Yes, I did.

SMITTY: Holy Toledo Constantine! If that ain't somethin else!

CONSTANTINE: Now then, does anyone here wish to conduct their own investigation with a question for one of our suspects? (*best to field at least 5 questions or more - and then cut it off with: And ONE more question. Single to Smitty by scratching nose.*)

SMITTY: I gotta question inspector, how were you so certain this wasn't some crazy accident? Huh? Like Mack was saying before. No one got the hot seat from the microphone before Sue was singing. And it checked out after she sang.

CONSTANTINE: I had considered that for quite a while. Until the letter.

SMITTY: Right! The letter.

ACT II

CONSTANTINE: She was giving someone the "brush off". And then it just so happens there's a convenient malfunction of wiring while she's singing. Coincidence? I think not. We're now looking into the eyes of malicious intent.

SMITTY: Gotcha! Sue gives somebody the brush off and they give her the kiss off.

CONSTANTINE: Touche!

SMITTY: Oh and one more detail Inspector, how did you figure out who it was?

CONSTANTINE: Well, after I allowed the questions, I addressed the parties involved... (*to cast -they un-freeze*) I need a moment or two of introspection here, to consider the case at hand. I believe I'm on the verge of cracking this perplexing affair. And the "affair" being a very key word. One of you, had a special relationship with the deceased. And because of a perceived indiscretion and a broken heart, exacted revenge. Pure and simple.

LELU: Well, that leaves me out.

CONSTANTINE: I will not leave anyone out! In fact, I will involve everyone.

STU: Wait! You what?

CONSTANTINE: I would be most curious to learn what the crowd has to say. I'd like to match it against my own theory. I have a very strong suspicion, but I'd like to see what they suspect. Who among you mugs is most likely to "take the fall"?

STU: Take the fall? Did he say, take the fall? I ain't taking nuthin' copper! This guy is off the cob! Lettin' them mugs ask us questions. Now he wants them to pin this rap on one of us!

LELU: What are you so punchy about Stu?

ACT II

STU: Punchy? Wait! Who's punchy? Me? No siree bob! Everything's swell! I got nuthin' to worry about.

MACK: Looks like *they* will be the judge of that.

STU: Shut your clam Gertrude.

MACK: My name's Mack fella. The Gertrude bit is gettin' old!

CONSTANTINE: Very well, as I said. I would be most interested in what our crowd thinks. Which of these individuals spreads the most suspicion? I would like to take a vote, if you will. (- *adapt Constantine dialogue to explain any voting methods you wish*)

   -*after the votes or other, continue with:*

JEAN-PAUL: S'il vous plaît! Monsieur Inspector! We must continue with the evening. If you could, how you say.. "Shake a leg"!

LELU: And how! That would be aces with me!

CONSTANTINE: Very good. I'll "shake my legs" at once. Let me begin by telling you that I found something slightly puzzling about this letter from Sugar Sandy..

MACK: Sweet Sue! For the love of Pete!

CONSTANTINE: I'm not certain it was Pete that she loved. But I am certain there was a strange way that she indicated who the letter was for. (*takes out letter*) Of course, a name would have been helpful. Had she simply scribbled To Jean-Paul or to Mr. John Smith or Fibber Magee... but she didn't.

LELU: Of course not!

MACK: Nope.

STU: Too easy.

JEAN-PAUL: No, no!

ACT II

LELU: Why would she?

CONSTANTINE: However, I believe she may have been indicating a particular person by using a symbol.

STU: A cymbal? Like on the drums?

JEAN-PAUL: It was a musician?

CONSTANTINE: No, I mean a symbol as in a trademark, a sign.

At first, I thought it was a simple character of some sort.

LELU: That would be Stu. He's a simple character.

MACK: You shred it wheat!

CONSTANTINE: But, upon closer inspection, I see it's a crude drawing of what appears to be a sword or perhaps a "knife".

MACK: A what?

STU: A sword?

CONSTANTINE: Or perhaps a knife!

JEAN-PAUL: A knife? What name is zis?

LELU: Why sure! That's our creepy German friend here! He's pretty handy with cuttin' people up.

BODYGUARD: Nine! Nine! (*takes out hatchet*) Is no sword!

STU: Naw, Hans don't use no knife. One-Eyed Joey uses a knife. Short Leg Murray uses a knife.

LELU: I thought Short Leg used an Ice Pick.

STU: Sometimes. In cooler weather. On odd-numbered days.

CONSTANTINE: If I may continue? At first, I couldn't understand what a knife may mean.

ACT II

MACK: It means you should cut out the malarkey and get to the point pal.

CONSTANTINE: I'm getting there! The point, no pun intended, is this letter, "sparked" a jilted lover to wish harm as it were. Maybe, they only meant to "stun" Sweet Suzy. It would look like a slight malfunction. But, the voltage was quite strong! Added to the fact that she was barefoot, Suzy became quite conductive. A human conduit of electricity.

LELU: We got that Constantine! We know! We're waitin' for the other shoe to drop! Who is this "Knife"?

CONSTANTINE: Yes, yes. The knife. I believe you Miss Lelu have a tattoo of a knife on your right shoulder blade!

LELU: How on Earth did you...

CONSTANTINE: (*interrupting*)And I believe you harbored a twinge of animosity toward the Sweet singing girl, did you not?

LELU: Well... I... perhaps maybe... just a teeny bit, but..

CONSTANTINE: But you didn't expect the voltage to be that strong did you? Just a little shock may have sent her on her way and...

(They Freeze as Smitty speaks)

SMITTY: Hey! Hang on a second! I don't remember Lelu taken the fall for this. That ain't what I got down here in my notes!

CONSTANTINE: It's not?

SMITTY: No!

CONSTANTINE: Of course, it's not!

(they un-freeze and as if starting over)

LELU: We got that Constantine! We know! We're waitin' for the other shoe to drop! Who is this "Knife"?

ACT II

CONSTANTINE: Yes, yes. The knife! (*cross to Truffaut*) If I am not mistaken Mr. Truffaut, before you were the Master of Ceremonies here at Chez Mort, you were in fact.. the Chef!

TRUFFAUT: Oui! But.. how you say...

CONSTANTINE: I say you were quite handy with a knife, were you not?

SMITTY: No, he was not.

TRUFFAUT: No I am not.

CONSTANTINE: Of course he wasn't! (*crosses away - looks at BODYGUARD*) But our foreign friend... you have a way with cutlery and maybe.... it wasn't him either was it?

SMITTY: Nope.

CONSTANTINE: Well, heck!

SMITTY: I can show you my notes..

CONSTANTINE: Notes! That's it! Music! I remember!

LELU: We got that Constantine! We know! We're waitin' for..

CONSTANTINE: (*interrupts*) Yes! Yes! I know, I know! The knife! (*beat*) This *knife* is, in reality, a *pet name* for someone here.

LELU: Ya mean like.. Lovey Dove?

CONSTANTINE: Yes. "Knife" maybe a crude allusion to someone's existing name.

STU: An illusion to a name? How do ya figure?

CONSTANTINE: I figure since our victim was versed in music, perhaps it is in music, we will find the answer.

MACK: What music?

ACT II

CONSTANTINE: Oh something like the song.. "Die Moritat von Mackie Messer".

STU: Dee Morty who's its?

BODYGUARD: Yah! Is from *Die Dreigroschenoper*[1]

STU: Gesundheit my friend.

LELU: Wait a second! Mackie Messer?! Sure! I know that tune! It's from that show! That Penny show!

CONSTANTINE: Yes. That would be *Three Penny Opera*, Miss Lelu. By Brecht and Weil.

STU: While? How about *while* we're still young! Tell us cause, I still don't get it.

JEAN-PAUL: So this "knife" is...how you say?

MACK: I think he's about to say me. I don't have time to stand around and find out. See you all in funny papers.

MACK turns and begins to exit quite quickly.

CONSTANTINE: Stop that man! Stop him at once!

STU *snaps his fingers and Bodyguard runs and grabs MACK.*

LELU: Why sure! A knife! *Mack* the Knife! It was Mack!

JEAN-PAUL: Qui est-ce?

CONSTANTINE: Even though he's no electrician, the stage manager would have had access to the wiring and the knowledge to create a little short circuit.

MACK: Says you, Constantine! You can't pinch me for this one.

CONSTANTINE: Oh but I think I can. I'm sure further investigations could tie you the victim quite nicely. I'm sure Mr. Jean-Paul can fill in a few details he has been hiding.

ACT II

JEAN-PAUL: I don't know. I have nothing to..

CONSTANTINE: I'm sure a revoked Nightclub license for harboring such criminal elements as Big Suit Stu and Hans the Hatchet, the dangerous Russian...

LELU: German.

CONSTANTINE: ..German, could change your mind.

JEAN-PAUL: Well, oh, Oui! Of course, I maybe know Mack was how you say... sweet on Sweet Sue and suddenly not sweet to Sue when Sue was sweet for the Stu..

CONSTANTINE: Yes, yes, yes. I'll need it all down in writing. Come along everyone. I will need statements from all of you. I need you all outside, you'll find my officers waiting..

STU: Hey wait a second!

CONSTANTINE: No waiting Mr Stu. I believe that to be an unregistered firearm you have on your person. And unless your Russian friend is gathering firewood, we will need to see about his axe.

They all exit the stage engaged in conversation -such as Stu Still complaining about going. Jean-Paul complaining about having a "show to get on with" etc... a cacophony of voices as they all exit.

CONSTANTINE: Well Smitty. That was pretty much the long and short of it. Of course, some of the details may be bit sketchy as well as the names. But there's your story.

SMITTY: Quite a story inspector. Thanks. Oh and just one detail.. about the names. Just so you know, my name isn't Smitty.

CONSTANTINE: It's not?

SMITTY: It's just a pen name, for the paper. My real name is Larry.

ACT II

CONSTANTINE: Larry?

SMITTY: Yep. Larry Dove. Thanks inspector, got to get this to press. See ya round. (*exits*)

CONSTANTINE: Yes. By all means, get it to press! The pen is mightier than the sword! (*thinks a moment -pulls Sweet Sue letter out of his pocket.*) Sword? Hmmm. (*beat*) Larry Dove? That almost kinda sounds like.. Lovey..(*beat*) Oh heck! Hey! Wait a minute! (*running off after Smitty*) Just a second! Smitty! Come back here!

The End

---

1. Dee Dry gro shin o per

DEATH NEAR DEAD MAN'S HOLLER

A MURDER MYSTERY COMEDY PLAY

Dedicated to my Grandfather, Leo W. Buck, who taught me to love Western movies, horses, small towns, and most important to keep it simple and honest. He also taught me how to shoot.

I am aware that my name has been connected with all the bank robberies in the country; but positively I had nothing to do with any one of them. I look upon my life since the war as a blank, and will never say anything to make it appear otherwise.

— COLE YOUNGER

My pistols, however, I always kept by me.

— JESSE JAMES

Fast is fine, but accuracy is everything. In a gun fight... You need to take your time in a hurry.

— WYATT EARP

CHARACTERS

JOEY STARRETT - *Young kid. Fascinated by outlaws and one day hopes to learn to shoot*

SHERIFF JOHN FORD - *Easy going sheriff of a small town where nothing much ever happens*

MRS PEACOCK - *conservative righteous Citizen. President of the Meridosa Ethics Ladies Guild*

SADIE MAE HARLOW: *Saloon girl/ entertainer with a heart of Gold.*

PARSON GRAHAM: *Town Spiritual leader*

DOC WATSON: *High educated medical professional who is currently on the wagon*

MISS CRABTREE - *the School teacher*

WILLIAM WESLEY JAMES -*aka Billy The Weasel aka Kid Vicious - stranger in town -former outlaw*

STRANGER -*an extra - seen in the saloon and other places*

SETTING - A small Mid-Western Town in the Late 1890's - various areas of the stage are representational of areas: Sheriff's office (upstage Left), Saloon (Upstate Right) and Streets (downstage center)

ACT ONE

❦

JOEY runs onto stage very excited - in street area -looking around.

JOEY: Sheriff! Sheriff Ford! (*crosses to other side*) Sheriff!

SHERIFF FORD enters

SHERIFF: Well howdy there Joey! What's all the commotion?

JOEY: Sheriff! I just got wind of some mighty fearful news!

SHERIFF: You don't say! Let me guess, old man Brennan's cow kicked the fence down and got loose in the garden again?

JOEY: No Sheriff!

SHERIFF: Doc Watson fell off the wagon and passed out in the horse trough.

JOEY: No Sheriff, it's not that! It's...

SHERIFF: Timmy Martin fell down the well and his dog came to fetch ya?

ACT ONE

JOEY: No Sheriff. Nuthin' like that! It's worse! I was just over to the Hawks ranch by Dead Man's Holler and I heard tell that none other than... Sergio Van Cleef is headed this way!

SHERIFF: Sergio Van Cleef?!!

JOEY: Yes! Ornery Eyes his-self!

SHERIFF: *(mock surprise)* Ya don't say!

JOEY: Sure as shootin! That's what the fellers was sayin! The meanest gunslinger to ever sling a gun is headed here to Meridosa! I heard he shot a man in St Joe just to watch him die! What are we gunna do Sheriff? What are we gunna do?

SHERIFF: Hmmmm. *(few beat thinking)* Well, nuthin I can do. .

JOEY: That's what I thought! We'll get the .. wait! Did you say... *nuthin?*

SHERIFF: Yep. I sure did.

JOEY: But... but... but Sheriff! What are ya.. ! How can ya...! Shouldn't ya be fixin ta round up a posse! That's what ya always do! I mean, ya always do sumthin! Why, when Frank Miller and his bunch was headed this way, you rounded up the boys and headed ta meet him over at the train station! And when that Edward's girl went missin', you rounded up Captain Clayton and that half injun Pawley and went searchin'! Ya always do sumthin! I cain't believe ya ain't doin nuthin'!

SHERIFF: Hold your horses there little buckaroo, let me explain. You see Joey, I...

MRS PEACOCK stomps on. She carries an Ear Trumpet (old time hearing device). She has to point it up to the person speaking in order to hear clearly -which she does not always do.

PEACOCK: Sheriff Ford! Sheriff John Ford! Oh! There you are!

SHERIFF: *(sighs)* Why afternoon Mrs. Peacock.

ACT ONE

PEACOCK: Yes, perhaps. Sheriff Ford, I have it under good authority, that new young woman employed at the libation hall of ill fame is a *trollop*! I received a correspondence from my dear sister in Dodge City and she informed me that this young woman, this Sadie Mae Harlow is of questionable repute. I demand that something be done!

JOEY: Mrs. Peacock! The sheriff ain't got time for this..

PEACOCK: You hold your tongue you young heathen! Sheriff, I will not idly sit by while this town turns it's conscience to the shade! As president of the Meridosa Ethics Ladies Guild auxiliary post 47 and recreational bridge league, I insist this Sadie Mae be put on the very next stagecoach out of town. *(beat)* Well? Why are you just standing there?

SHERIFF: I don't mean to get your feathers all ruffled Mrs. Peacock, but as far as I know, Sadie Mae Harlow is a Dance hall girl. Nothin' more. She's an entertainer.

PEACOCK: Tamer is right! She needs *taming*, just like a shrew!

SHERIFF: No, no. *Entertainer*. Sadie Mae is an ENTERTAINER..

PEACOCK: Entertainer?! Ha! And we all know what entertainers are like! These so-called people of the theatrical persuasion, prancing about on the stage saying "Look at me Look at me!" You can't fool me, Sheriff!

SHERIFF: What would you have me do?

PEACOCK: Do? I told you what you need to do! Tell her to be on her way!

SHERIFF: If I recall Mrs. Peacock, you wanted Miss Dallas to leave town for exposing her ankle in public.

ACT ONE

Truth was.. she had a mosquito bite and was simply scratching it. And last week, you wanted Miss Crabtree, the school teacher run out on a rail for indecency and lewd behavior.

PEACOCK: Why she was parading around in a flimsy dressing gown!

SHERIFF: What you failed to say is that Miss Crabtree was *in her home* and you were looking through her window! And while we're at it, you can forget your tar and feather petition for old Mose Harper! Whistling on a Tuesday is not a crime! Least not around these parts.

PEACOCK: Well I find it offensive!

SHERIFF: And I find this all very tiring Mrs. Peacock. I think you best be on your way now.

JOEY: Yea Mrs. Peacock! Me and the Sheriff have more important things to talk about. The fact that Sergio Van Cleef is headed our way! The meanest, baddest, orneriest hornswaggler to ever breathe the light of day! Why there's bound to be shootin' and folks dying all over the town! A real bloodbath!

PEACOCK: I'll say there will be a wrath! Why I never! Allowing a man of such low moral standards just to waltz into our town! Not to mention what it will do to property values! It's bad enough our good town has to be situated near a valley shamefully named after a dead man! No wonder such foul things occur here...

SHERIFF: Now Mrs. Peacock, you know that's not true! Dead Man's Holler was named after Arthur Redmon! It was Redmon's Hollow! But folk just got to pronouncin' it wrong and it stuck! But folks just hear what they want and say what they will!

PEACOCK: Well I'll say something! Something should be done, you hear? Do something Sheriff! Such as your duty! You are an elected official! It's your duty to serve and protect the citizens!

ACT ONE

JOEY: She's right! Ya gotta do somethin! Hey! I know! You could deputize *me* Sheriff! I'm pert near old enough. I can handle a gun. I just need someone to teach how to shoot!

SHERIFF: Listen you two, what I been fixin to say is... I know Van Cleef is headed to town. I've known for days.

PEACOCK: Fort Hayes? I'm talking about here in Meridosa!

SHERIFF: No, no! I said *days*. FOR DAYS!

PEACOCK: For four days? That is a blatant miscarriage of justice! You may turn in your badge at anytime Sheriff! (*holds her hand out*)

SHERIFF: Now don't go gettin' your dander in a tizzy! What I'm saying is that Van Cleef is *supposed* to be headin' to Meridosa! He's under custody of the Marshall from over in Peckinpah county. . He'll be locked up over at the jail. There's nuthin to fret over.

JOEY: Our Jail? How long a spell?

SHERIFF: Maybe a day. Maybe two. He's taking him over to the train depot. They're catching the 3:10 to Yuma.

JOEY: You mean..? He ain't comin here to shoot up the town? Rob the bank? Nuthin?

SHERIFF: Nope. They'll be no more shootin and robbin for Van Cleef.

JOEY: Well dern! That's disappointin'!

PEACOCK: Appointing? I'll say there will be an *appointing*! Appointing a new Sheriff! A notorious outlaw taking residence in our town? Shameful! And for another thing, you never looked in on that rapscallion pilfering around my property! I informed you about it last week!

SHERIFF: I know and I was fixing to..

ACT ONE

PEACOCK: I'm most certain he was there last night. A Peeping Parker! I heard my shed door opening and closing. This morning my milk pail was moved out behind the barn! Just wait till the Ethics Guild hears about your lack of duty! This town is headed to hades in a handbasket!

MRS PEACOCK Storms off

JOEY: Boy, Peacock sure gets a bee in her bonnet 'bout things don't she?

SHERIFF: Yessir Joey, she can be a bag of nails sometimes. Been that way since she lost her husband.

JOEY: Her husband? What happened? Was he gunned down?

SHERIFF: No, she just *lost* him. (*beat*) They went over to the General Store one day; she went to look at fabric, he went to look for a coal scuttle and well.... never saw him again. There was an old Chuck line rider said he saw someone who looked like Mr. Peacock - a high tailin' toward the county line.

JOEY: Can't rightly blame him fer cuttin a path outta town. Seems she blames everybody for pert near everythin'. She even tried to get your goat about Sadie and Ornery Eyes comin ta town.

SHERIFF: Speakin' a which, I best be headed over to the Jail. The Marshall and his party should be here anytime. (*squints looking up*) Yep, Looks to be 'bout high noon.

JOEY: Can I go with ya Sheriff? Can I? I never saw a *real* outlaw before! And like I said, I know how ta handle a gun! My paw showed me!

SHERIFF: Naw, you best be headin' home Joey. Yer mom's gunna be worried.

JOEY: Aw con-sarn-it! Can you at least teach how ta shoot sometime?

ACT ONE

SHERIFF: Maybe later, Joey. Maybe later. You get on home now.

SHERIFF exits

JOEY: OK.

JOEY watches Sheriff leaves. He stands for a moment looking around. Then looks straight ahead. He drops his arms to his sides and wiggles his fingers as if he is in a showdown. Ready to reach for his gun.

JOEY: (*as if addressing outlaw*) All right Vallance. I warned ya! You maybe the toughest hombre south of the picket wire, but I told ya - this here town ain't big enough for the both of us. On the count of three. One... Two...

WOMAN VOICE (*Off Stage*) Joseph! Joseph Starrett!

JOEY: Awww! Con-sarn-it ma!

JOEY slumps - and exits

Lights fade or transition music - Saloon piano type of music plays - STRANGER walks into Saloon and sits at table. Pulls hat down low as if to hide his face.

SADIE MAE enters through crowd perhaps speaking to audience as if they are patrons at the Saloon - she comes up to stage area - PARSON GRAHAM enters

SADIE: Why Parson Graham! Fancy seeing you in here!

PARSON: Good day Miss Harlow.

SADIE: And what brings you into the Parched Persimmon?

PARSON: Well, since I wasn't counting on seeing you in the church anytime soon, I thought I'd pay you a visit.

SADIE: Oh ye of little faith!

PARSON: Faith is the substance of things hoped for, the evidence of things not seen.

ACT ONE

SADIE: And since you haven't *seen* me in church, you *hoped* to find me here? Aren't you worried the town folk will spot you in here in the saloon? What would Mrs. Peacock say?

SADIE briefly interacts with Stranger silently

PARSON: Actually, that's what I came to see you about. As you know, Mrs. Peacock is head of the Meridosa Ethics Ladies Guild..

SADIE: And they want me to join?

PARSON: No, Miss Harlow..

SADIE: Please, call me Sadie Mae.

SADIE gets bottle and glass – takes to Stranger

PARSON: As you wish, Sadie Mae. What I'm here to.. well, inform you.. is about Mrs Peacock. Seems she's been making the rounds.

SADIE: I know Parson. The rounds she's been making have made it squarely to me. Seems she has some concerns about my character. Let me tell you, she has a lot of gumption spreading such hogwash about me. I'm a dance hall girl, Parson. My calling is entertainment! That's it! I'm working my way back east for a career on the stage. What's so sinful about singing and dancing?

PARSON: Well the thing is.. Mrs Peacock and her committee tend to hold establishments such as this in low regard.

SADIE: I know. I've dealt with her kind before. I knew her sister, Miss Gulch in Dodge city. The apple doesn't fall far from the tree.

PARSON: I just wanted you to know that Mrs. Peacock can be a force in which to be reckoned. When she gets something her mind, whether it be right or wrong.. well, she wields quite a bit of influence in this town.

ACT ONE

SADIE: Has she influenced you? Are you here to tell me to pack my bags and leave?

PARSON: No Sadie, I'm not here to do anything of the sort. I just want you to be prepared for the wrath she is attempting to bring.

SADIE: Let her bring her wrath!. Same reason I got out of Dodge. I didn't like the piano player they had. Had no sense of tempo and his middle C was flat. I plan to be out of here in a year.

STRANGER puts down coins on table and exits

PARSON: Very well Sadie. I wish you all the best. I guess I better be heading on. *(turns to exit)* Oh one more thing, if you are interested, I do have a need for a strong voice in the church choir. And I'm quite certain the middle C on our piano is in tune.

SADIE: *(chuckles)* I'll think about it, Parson. And thanks for... looking out for me.

PARSON: It's what I do.

SADIE: And I'll be fine with the Peacock wrath. After all, what does the good book say... if the Big Guy is for us, who can be against us.

PARSON: Yes. It does say that. Romans. 8:31 in fact.

MISS PEACOCK quickly enters is carrying a rifle. She does not have her hearing device.

PARSON GRAHAM quickly intervenes - moving in-between Peacock and Sadie

PARSON: Mrs. Peacock! Please! We do not resort to these levels! Put that weapon away!

ACT ONE

PEACOCK: Why should I? A citizen has a right to protect themselves! It's my right as set down in our great Declaration of Independence!

SADIE: Actually Peacock, it's the *Constitution*. The second amendment.

PEACOCK: Your second what?

SADIE: *Amendment!* There's another amendment that says; everyone is guaranteed due process of law. Not by a crazy old witch with a gun!

PEACOCK: What do you mean *which gun?* Why the one I have right here!

Brings up barrel pointing it at Sadie. PARSON quickly reaches out and pushes it down

PARSON: Remember my teaching on Sunday! For with what judgment ye judge, ye shall be judged: and with what measure ye meet, it shall be measured to you again!

PARSON takes rifle away from Peacock

PEACOCK: I'm meeting measures to protect myself

from peepin parkers traipsing around my home! That and murderous criminal elements our Sheriff invites to town!

PARSON: Murderous criminal elements?

PEACOCK: Relevance? What do you mean? It's perfectly *relevant!* That desperado Van Cleavage is coming!

SADIE: Sergio *Van Cleef?*

PEACOCK: The Sheriff has no right letting a villainous brigand to set foot in our town. It's bound to draw all sorts of undesirables.

SADIE: Oh P'shaw! Van Cleef ain't so bad.

64

ACT ONE

PEACOCK: Say! Just a moment! How do *you* know this hooligan?! Is he one of your *associates*?

SADIE: Hardly. I saw him a time or two in Dodge. He's more notorious than the James boys or the Daltons! Everyone knows him!

PEACOCK: Owes him?! I don't owe him anything! And leave it to someone like you to know about such a nefarious person! Parson Graham, I am shocked that you are here associating with this heathen! I demand you explain yourself.

PARSON: Well, I was merely...

SADIE: (*speaks loudly*) The Parson was here to recruit me for the CHURCH CHOIR.

PEACOCK: Church Choir? You? Land a Goshen! That'll be the day!

SADIE: (singing) *Amazing Grace, how sweet the sound..*

PEACOCK: First our town welcomes outlaws and now our church welcomes Calico Queens! Surely it must be the end times!

DOC WATSON enters

DOC: Greetings to one and all on this splendid day of monkeyshines and charivari! (*shevaree*)

SADIE: Oh look! It's one of the four horsemen now!

DOC: Oh Contrair Sadie Mae! I haven't a horse but an old pack mule! I doubt I shall spread much pestilence upon its sorry gallop.

PEACOCK: Land sakes! Such indecency!

DOC: Speaking of indecency Miss Harlow, I fear my eyes are playing vile tricks upon me. I imagine that I am seeing the

ACT ONE

Parson and Peacock standing here in the Saloon! Please tell me it's but a mirage.

PARSON: It's quite *real* Doc.

PEACOCK: Suffering barrel fever no doubt!

DOC: Great Caesar's Ghost! The illusion doth speak!

DOC reaches out and touches PEACOCK'S face to make sure she is real.

PEACOCK: I'll kindly ask you to refrain from touching my person.

DOC: Forgive me Peacock. I was just checking your face. It seems to be absent of the spectacles I prescribed for your vision. And where's your hearing horn?

PEACOCK: Clearing corn? Ha! The only corn anyone's been clearing is the *corn* whiskey from a jug Doctor! Filled to the gills with scamp juice!

DOC: I'll have you know my good woman, I haven't touched a drop of anti-fogmatic in years. uh.. months.. days! The medical profession requires nerves of precision! Bottled courage is not for me! Old Doc has taken a holiday from the fermented substance. (*goes up close to Peacock with loud voice*) I'M ON THE WAGON!

PEACOCK: Ha! Then explain yourself. Why are you *here* in the saloon!? Did you fall from your wagon as it was rolling by?

DOC: Why am I...? Uh...(*to himself*) Why am I here? (*beat*) Well, I... possessed a hankering for some of that fine Sarsaparilla that's served up here. With a dash of cherry no less. And may I ask why *you* are here? And Parson Graham, my good sir, why are you in possession of that thunder stick?

SADIE: It belongs to Peacock! She's taking her constitutional.

ACT ONE

DOC: I see! Well, be of the most care with that Peacock. You could spoil someone's day. It's all fun and games until someone's mortal coil gets shrugged off!

PEACOCK: Hmmp! You're as crooked as a Virginia fence! A disgrace to the medical profession.

DOC: And what do you hear from Mr. Peacock these days?

SADIE: (*sings*) *I once was lost.. but now I'm found...*

DOC: Still hasn't turned up, has he? MR PEACOCK?

PEACOCK: I don't have to stand here and be insulted by the likes of you.

DOC: No, I'm sure you could be insulted most anywhere Peacock. And by the likes of most anyone.

PEACOCK: The Ethics Guild will be hearing about this matter! After I report the sheriff for his miscarriage of justice! Allowing barbarians to lodge in our city! Parson Graham, if you would kindly see after my safety? I would like some words with you.

PARSON: By all means.

PEACOCK: I bid you and your like, good day!

PEACOCK stomps off. PARSON follows her off.

DOC: Alas, some people give us pleasure when they arrive, and others when they leave.

SADIE: Well, Doc. What will it be? The usual?

DOC: Usual? Oh no, no! I am quite serious. I'm on the straight and narrow. Say you got any more of that fine sarsaparilla?

SADIE: Why Doc Watson! You are serious!

DOC: Quite so, my dear. Quite so.

ACT ONE

SADIE: Well, right this way *(they continue on Doc sits at table Sadie gets Sarsaparilla)*

JOEY runs back out on stage in street area down stage. He is looking in the distance as if watching something.

JOEY: *(pointing to distance)* Hey! It's the posse! Hey everyone! They're here!

MISS CRABTREE enters looking in distance also.

CRABTREE: What is it, Joseph? What are you saying?

JOEY: Why, hello Miss Crabtree. You sure look lovely today.

CRABTREE: Why thank you, Joseph. So, who are those people over there?

JOEY: Why yonder is the Sheriff and the bunch from Peckinpah County.

CRABTREE: Oh. Yes, I see our Sheriff but... I not familiar with those other men.

JOEY: Well, the tall feller in the group is the Marshall. And the rest is his posse.

CRABTREE: Marshall?

JOEY: Yes mam. Marshall Tucker. Can't ya see?

CRABTREE: What are the Marshall and those men doing here?

JOEY: Well, you see that feller they have bound up on that horse? That's the outlaw Sergio Van Cleef. Ol' Ornery Eyes. Most notorious six-gun in the land! *(a few beats as he watches)* I thought he'd be taller. He looked taller on the wanted poster.

CRABTREE: So tell me, Joseph, why are they bringing him here?

ACT ONE

JOEY: The Sheriff's lettin' them keep him at the jail for a spell. Just till they catch the train outta town.

DOC WATSON wanders down from Saloon area.

DOC: Greetings and salutations to our cherished School madam and young Joseph. *(looks in distance where their attention is directed)* Say, what commotion carries on over there?

JOEY: It's a posse from Peckinpah County.

DOC: Peckinpah posse? I must say that's a wild bunch! They must be the contingent that's transporting the marauder Van Cleef!

CRABTREE: That's what Joseph was just telling me. I must say, keeping a person like *that* in our town who is.. deplorable, villainous and wicked! It's rather exciting, isn't it? *(beat)* I mean, as a *learning* experience, of course. *(to Joey)* You see what happens to men like that Joseph? No good will ever come from leaning outside of the law.

JOEY: I know Miss Crabtree but.. they don't write no good adventure stories about people leaning inside the law!

DOC: I heard he shot a man in Fort Smith just to witness the demise. I remembered him being taller.

JOEY: You mean to say you know Ornery Eyes?

DOC: For a moment. Back in Abilene when I was first practicing the medical arts. Treated him for a green mesquite thorn he acquired in his posterior region. Never did render to me the currency owed. Took off in the dead of night with two bottles of my finest medicinal tonic and three silver spoons.

CRABTREE: The nerve of some people.

DOC: Oh and.. the wife. I almost forgot. Took my wife as well.

CRABTREE: He took your wife?

ACT ONE

DOC: Stoic woman. Full of spirit and determination. Or should I say *irritation*? I had but one nerve remaining and she trod upon it daily. Such a shame, I sorely missed those spoons. Had to eat soup with a ladle for a week.

MRS PEACOCK enters - with her hearing horn

PEACOCK: Which one is the no count skunk?

DOC: Take your pick Peacock. But I assure you, I bathed this morning.

PEACOCK: Mind your puns and quips Doctor, I'm talking about the men over there.

JOEY: You mean Ornery Eyes? They're takin' him through the door now! He's the man in black.

PEACOCK: The man in *back*? The tall one?

JOEY: No, that's the Marshall. The man in BLACK!

PEACOCK: Naturally. Black is the shade of evil!

DOC: Black can be very slimming if one's taking on a few pounds.

CRABTREE: And it goes well with most anything.

JOEY: I thought for sure there'd be shootin! Like in that one story where they tried to lock up Joe Burdette! There was all kinds of shootin' and blood spillin'.

CRABTREE: Joseph Alan Starrett! Such talk for a lad! You shouldn't be filling your mind with such stories! You should be reading decent stories... like Jules Verne or something light, like Dostoevsky! Better yet, brushing up on your addition skills.

JOEY: Aw Miss Crabtree, I know how to cipher real good.

PEACOCK: Cider? I could go for some good cider myself.

ACT ONE

DOC: Yes, being a busybody certainly makes one a tad parched.

DOC exits

PEACOCK: And where's that Parson with my means of protection? I'm going to need it. There's bound to be all sorts of heinous and pernicious elements coming this way! Invite the devil in and his minions are soon to follow!

PEACOCK exits

CRABTREE: And I have a lesson plan in which to attend. Joseph, don't forget there will be a Grammer test in the morning.

JOEY: I aint gunna forget.

CRABTREE: You "won't" forget.

JOEY: No ma'am. That neither.

CRABTREE exits.

JOEY: 'Sides. It weren't as excitin' as I thought it'd be. Thought Ornery Eyes would be ... well, ornery. *(beat)* Con sarn it anyways. Best go tend to my cipherin' and grammerin'.

JOEY starts to exit and then stops and turns

JOEY: *(cont - as if addressing outlaw)* What did you say Ike Clanton? Oh yea? Well I warned ya! This here corral ain't big enough for the both of us. OK?

BILL WESLEY enters in slightly behind JOEY -out of his vision

JOEY: On the count of three. You just go ahead a drew. One... Two...

BILLY: Three!

JOEY jumps -turning quickly.

ACT ONE

JOEY: Ah! Dag burn mister! Ya scared the tar outta me! Ya oughta not be sneakin' up on a folk like that!

BILLY: Sorry little cowpoke. I couldn't resist.

JOEY: *(looking Billy Over)* You ain't from around here are ya?

BILLY: Nope. Sure ain't.

JOEY: Well what brings to town?

BILLY: Whiskey boat. Caught it up north. Rode it down river.

JOEY: Are you visitin somebody here?

BILLY: Might be I am. Might be I ain't. And it might be I'm just fixin to rest a bit in this one dog town. Tell me, you know where a fella might find a nice game of faro or poker 'round these parts?

JOEY: Some of the fellas play over to the Saloon. The Parched Persimmon. It's right down yonder, next to Big Nose Kate's Dry Goods.

BILLY: Much obliged to ya.

JOEY: *(studies Billy for a moment)* Say mister.. you look a might familiar... have I seen you somewheres?

BILLY: Seen me? I said I ain't from around here.

JOEY: What's your name?

BILLY: Name? I don't need no stinkin' name.

JOEY: No name? A man with *no* name? That's a might funny.

BILLY: Is it? *(sighs)* I had one for a bit. The one my ma give me when I was born. She gave me a name so that I'd know she was talkin to me.

JOEY: Yea? So what name did she give ya?

ACT ONE

BILLY: William Wesley James. Called me William for a spell being all proper. Most time she called me *Kid*. Hey Kid! Get down from there! Wash ya hands for supper Kid. Other folks called me Bill or Billy. That's why I don't care much for names. Too dag many of 'em to keep track.

JOEY: William Wesley..*(thinking)* Kid. *(beat)* Billy? Of course! That's where I heard of you! Some call you Billy the.. *(stops himself)*.

BILLY: You be mindful how you finish that. Got a few names I don't rightly care for. Some of 'em stick in my craw. Make me a might vicious. Folks don't like it when I get vicious. Now, what were you gunna say?

JOEY: I was.. I was gunna say... that I gotta get home. Practicing my cipherin for school.

BILLY: Cipherin huh? Sound like you was doin a fine job a countin' when I walked up. Where was we? *(beat)* There was one...... two.....

BILL drops his hand and wiggles his fingers as if getting ready to draw his gun.

BILLY: What comes next? *(a few beats)* THREE!

JOEY runs off quickly in terror. BILL laughs and slowly exits

Lights down - transitional music -suggestion: "Big Iron" -Marty Robbins

SHERIFF enters sitting on chair and Desk

MUSIC FADES - Lights up

PARSON GRAHAM enters

PARSON: Afternoon Sheriff.

SHERIFF: Afternoon Parson. How can I help ya?

ACT ONE

PARSON: As you know it's my duty to provide console to any incarcerated souls here at the jail. Since we have a new prisoner, I thought I would see if requires my services.

SHERIFF: That's a kind of ya Parson, he's not *our* prisoner. He's belongs to the Marshall of Peckinpah county. But I'm sure he wouldn't mind. He and his boys is restin' up over at the Cartwright place.

PARSON: One other thing I believe you should be aware. Mrs. Peacock has assumed a somewhat vigilant attitude about this matter. She was wielding a rifle a while ago at the Saloon. I managed to liberate it from her and store it in a safe place.

SHERIFF: What in tarnation was she doing with that?

PARSON: I believe she thought the citizens should be protected. She has the impression that bringing Van Cleef to town invites evil. As it says in Matthew; a*n evil man out of the evil treasure bringeth forth evil things.*

SHERIFF: Well, I was afraid somethin' like this'd happen. Folks get to thinkin just havin a man like onary eyes settin here in the jail will invite every low life in surroundin area. That's just plain foolishness!

JOEY runs in

JOEY: Sheriff Ford! Sheriff Ford! Ya ain't gunna believe who's here! William Wesley James! Alias Kid Vicious! Alias Billy The Weasel! Just seen him! He talked to me!

SHERIFF: Kid Vicious? When? Where?

JOEY: I seen him across the way. He done snuck up behind me. Said he's was lookin' for a game a poker. I thought he looked familiar. Then I 'membered where'd I seen him! On that ol' poster right over yonder on your wall. And then he...

ACT ONE

SHERIFF: Slow down a minute Joey. Now, are you sure? You sure it's him?

JOEY: Sure as shootin it's him! He's the spit of that picture on the poster!

PARSON: Forgive me Sheriff but..who is William Wesley ?

SHERIFF: Kid Vicious was a member of the gang headed by the man we have locked up.

JOEY: Yea Parson! He was Ornery Eyes right hand man! Till the double-cross! They'd planned to hold up train near Wichita. But them Pinkerton boys was waiting on 'em. Van Cleef got word and with his cold feet ran off. Didn't warn Billy .

SHERIFF: And Billy walked right into 5 years at the Kansas State penn.

JOEY: You reckon he's here cause he knows Van Cleef is here? He's fixin to square things?

SHERIFF: There's no telling why he's here. Joey, I need you to run over the Cartwrights and fetch the Marshall and his boys. Let him know the Kid's in town.

JOEY: Sure will Sheriff!! (*JOEY runs off*)

PARSON: Anything I can do?

SHERIFF: Well Parson, I'm a bit short-handed here right now. I didn't quite figure word would spread so fast about our guest. I know you're a man of the cloth and not of the gun, but if you could hold down the fort here for a few minutes while I see to this.

PARSON: Certainly Sheriff. I'd be honored to serve.

SHERIFF: Oughta make it proper and deputize ya. Raise your right hand.

ACT ONE

Parson raises his right hand.

SHERIFF: Do you solemnly swear... well, of course, you don't. And uh.. do you ..I forget the words but... just say *I do.*

PARSON: I do.

SHERIFF: Good! You're a deputy! I have an old navy colt I keep 'round here that I can....

PARSON: No Sheriff. I'll be fine. *Not by might, nor by power. nor by guns.*

SHERIFF: That's the Spirit! I should be back shortly. If anyone asks tell them... I've gone over the livery stable to see about shoeing a new mare. (*SHERIFF exits*)

After a few beats Parson Graham walks over and sits.

PARSON: (*sings softly*) *Down in the valley, the valley so low. Hang your head over. Hear the wind blow...*

MISS CRABTREE enters

CRABTREE: Why Parson Graham, I didn't expect to find you here.

PARSON: (*stands*) Good afternoon Miss Crabtree.

CRABTREE: Where is Sheriff Ford?

PARSON: The Sheriff had to ..go see to see a man about a horse. Something I can help you with Miss Crabtree?

CRABTREE: Me? Oh no, I was just... curious. I understand there is a.. notorious man who ventured outside the law, taking residence here.

PARSON: Yes, mam. There is. Sheriff has him locked up in the back.

ACT ONE

CRABTREE: Oh good. I'm glad. Glad that he's... locked up all secure. It gives a girl.. a sense of.. of... well, security, knowing such matters.. that evil men such as the one in question is...

PARSON: Yes mam. He's locked up... all securely.. there in back.

As Crabtree begins dialogue below - Billy: (KID VICIOUS) should stroll down stage or through the audience looking around. He should do so rather quickly - not stealing too much focus.

CRABTREE: After all, what would this society be with men such as.. well, the one in question, if they were allowed to roam the streets?

PARSON: Yes. (*clears throat*) That's fine to know Miss Crabtree. Uh.. fine that you find peace with the situation. I hasten to say there are some people in town who are not as peaceful.

KID VICIOUS exits - As SHERIFF strolls in down stage - in same path as the KID as Crabtree speaks below:

CRABTREE: Yes, I know Parson. Just knowing that men like the Sheriff are here to protect us from plundering and pillaging and other.. unspeakable verbs. And of course, persons such yourself, who are available to tend to our spirits and pray for our souls so that we may soar like eagles and give us a... peaceful easy feeling.

PARSON: There are more things, that frighten us than injure us, and we suffer more in imagination than in reality.

CRABTREE: Is that from the Good Book?

PARSON: No ma'am, it's from another book. Gentleman named Seneca.

CRABTREE: I feel it is important to learn all one can. From different books and life. To experience many things. Speaking of which, do you think it would be possible.. just to take a peek at the prisoner? You know, just for the experience?

ACT ONE

PARSON: Now Miss Crabtree, I believe you should discuss that matter with the Sheriff. I can't in good conscience allow you back in the jail.

CRABTREE: But Parson do you realize how exciting something like this is? Nothing exciting ever happens in this town! This is a once in a lifetime opportunity and I don't care a continental about your conscience. Pardon my french! I sit all day teaching kids the many sights and wonders of the world, the heroes and the villains, the adventures of great explorers, all from a drafty old schoolhouse in the smallest town in the middle of nowhere!

PARSON: Miss Crabtree, I had no idea you felt so strongly about the situation.

CRABTREE: I apologize. *(sighs)* My nerves have been frayed since Mrs. Peacock caused that commotion by peeking in my window. *(beat -she begins walking away as if to exit - stops and turns)* Say, speaking of which, the jail cell has a window doesn't it?

PARSON: Window? I believe so. A small one around the back and..

CRABTREE: Thank you, Parson! *(she quickly exits)*

LIGHTS DOWN - *Transitional Music - Saloon Piano type - STRANGER enters Saloon sits.*

LIGHTS UP

BILLY walks into Saloon Area. SADIE MAE approaches him.

SADIE: Howdy stranger. Say, you're new in these parts aren't you?

BILLY: This town sure has folks full of wonder about new people and these parts.

SADIE: Amongst other things. What can I get for you?

ACT ONE

BILLY: I heard tell some of the fellers rounds here run a game a faro. Maybe some poker.

SADIE: Sometimes they do. Later in the evening. Do I know you from somewhere?

BILLY: Could be. I've been somewhere. If you've been somewhere, maybe we met.

SADIE: Maybe. I was thinking more like.. Dodge City.

BILLY: I'm thinkin' maybe.. you cut the thinkin' and the talking and fetch me somethin' to drink.

SADIE: I could do both. Whiskey?

BILLY: Whiskey don't agree with me. Tends to make me vicious.

SHERIFF enters.

SHERIFF: Well, well, well! Kid Vicious! Fancy seeing you in my town..

BILLY turns quickly as if ready to draw.

BILLY: I was wonderin' when you'd show.

SHERIFF: Is that right? Well, with Ornery Eyes also in town, I was wonderin' when *you* would show.

BILLY: Looks like we done solved our wonderin'. But ya see, Sheriff... I ain't wanted for nuthin. I done my stretch. Unlike some.

SHERIFF: Like *some* sittin' in my jail right now?

BILLY: Don't rightly care who you got settin' in your jail. I'm just passin through lookin for a friendly game of cards. And maybe some buttermilk or... cool clear water.

SHERIFF: Sadie? You want to get the gentleman here a cup of water.

ACT ONE

BILLY: Thank ya kindly Sheriff.

SADIE MAE crosses gets water for Billy. She can also interact with Stranger – getting a bottle and glass through dialogue below

SHERIFF: So, you're just in town for a game of cards, is that it?

BILLY: That's it. As you can plainly see.. (*opens coat*) Ain't armed. Ain't lookin for trouble. And I ain't had no one in 5 years call me "Kid".

SHERIFF: What do they call you now?

BILLY: Most time they just call me Sir. As in.. yes sir and no sir.

SHERIFF: How's the name Billy? Have any objections to that name?

BILLY: So long as it stops at *Billy*.

DOC WATSON enters.

DOC: (*sees Billy*) Jumpin' land o' Tarnation! Billy The Weasel!

BILLY: Like that right there! Now that just hurts my feelins somethin fierce!

SHERIFF: Well Doc, I take it you know this here gentleman?

DOC: I gathered his acquaintance upon helping a compadre of his with a sticky medical condition. And they were kind enough to assist me with clearing up the clutter in my silverware drawer.

SHERIFF: That's might neighborly of 'em.

DOC: Isn't though? Speaking of neighbors, there seems to be a matter with the Ethics League. As I was passing the General store, I noticed a gaggle of these League lasses purchasing pitchforks and other mob inspired objects. I believe they tend to do some farming with your guest over at the hoosegow. I may be going out on a limb but I believe there was a reference to the justice tree on the edge of town.

ACT ONE

SHERIFF: Well dag-gum-it! That's all I need right now. I better get over there and tend to it.

BILLY: You'd better Sheriff. Can't have no lawlessness in a nice town like this.

SHERIFF: And you better be doin' just what you say you came to do.

BILLY: Game of chance Sheriff. It's the only game I came to play.

SHERIFF: Speakin' of chance, any chance you could assist me Doc? They shouldn't be too hard to contend with beins Peacock ain't present.

DOC: Sure thing Sheriff.

SHERIFF and DOC Exit crossing down stage – STRANGER exits also

BILLY: *(to himself)* Ain't nuthin' in this life is a sure thing. 'Cept dyin'.

BILLY exits - As SHERIFF and DOC cross downstage JOEY runs in quickly.

JOEY: Sheriff! Sheriff Ford! I done told the Marshall! He and the boys will be headin back in two shakes of a lambs tail!

SHERIFF: Thank you Joey. You can run along home now and tend to your studies.

SHERIFF and DOC exit. JOEY stands for a moment watching them leave

JOEY: My studies? I know all there is ta know about important matters and such. *(reaches in back pocket and pulls out small folded pamphlet -dime western novel)* I study all about it in these here half dime books. There's Kit Carson. Jesse James. Curly Bill. Better readin' than any school book. *(sticks book back in pocket and starts to*

ACT ONE

exit but stops - speaks to imaginary foe) What did you say, stranger? *(beat)* My name? They call me Wild Joey Six Guns. But you might have heard me called The Meridosa Kid. *(beat)* Yep. That's right. *(beat)* Oh yea? Well, you'd better reach for 'em. On the count a three. *(drops his hand loosens his fingers)* One..... Two....... THREE!

JOEY quickly draws his imaginary gun being his index finger and thumb - just as he does we hear a GUNSHOT. - JOEY looks terrified for a second and then inspects his finger expecting to see gunsmoke rising. He backs up a few steps and then runs quickly off.

LIGHTS DOWN -transition music -Chorus of Streets Of Laredo (Cowboys Lament)

LIGHTS UP - SHERIFF stands in Office with DOC WATSON, PARSON in chair

DOC: Well Sheriff, if you were harboring any doubt, you might as well turn it out to sea, because he's not only merely dead, he's really most sincerely dead.

SHERIFF: Dead! I just can't imagine such a thing! It don't make sense Doc!

DOC: A man can die of all sorts of maladies and mishaps of biology.

SHERIFF: How can a man.. locked up in jail cell.. be dead? With no one around?

PARSON: Forgive me Sheriff, but there was *someone* around. I was here. The only thing I heard was Mr. Van Cleef. He called out, like a shriek and then I heard something fall. I went to see and.. there he was. Lying on the floor.

DOC: Perhaps he fell and hit his head. That would explain the wound on his right temple. But in my experience, a man falls and hits his head, it may render him unconscious but rarely is it fatal. We have quite a mystery on our hands.

ACT ONE

SHERIFF: Another mystery is – what I'm gunna tell the Marshall? He trusted me to keep the prisoner safe.

DOC: Until they could take him away and hang him? Seems to me you saved him both a trip and the trouble.

SHERIFF: Ornery Eyes was my responsibility. How am I gunna explain that he's lying dead in my jail? And 'sides that, nobody but a few people knew he was here.

DOC: I had the displeasure of knowing him. But I lack the hard feelings to carry out an execution or the ability to render myself invisible, slip into his cell and clobber him on the cranium.

SHERIFF: I do know of someone who knew him well and knew he was here. And carried a good reason to see him on the other side of the dirt. Doc, you and me have a few matters to sort out before we get the black Mariah to pick up one for the hill of boots.

PARSON: About the town folk Sheriff, do you think it wise to tell everyone?

SHERIFF: They're gunna find out one way or the other. Lettin the cat outta the bag's a whole lot easier than puttin' it back in. I know. I've tried.

PARSON: Sure thing Sheriff.

SHERIFF: Might as well get that cell cleared up. May have a Weasel to cage in it.

SHERIFF, PARSON AND DOC EXITS –

The next afternoon –

A few tables should be set in main stage area to represent Saloon. BILLY is seated playing Solitaire. SADIE MAE sits at the other table. Extra stranger with head down on table. MRS PEACOCK will enter (through crowd) speaking to audience.

ACT ONE

PEACOCK: I'll have you know this is the most disgraceful occurrence ever! Ladies of the guild, shall we stand idly by and subject ourselves to such miscarriage of justice?! No, I say! Allowing criminals to board in our town? Allowing peeping parkers to prance around your home at night? One has to fend for one's self!

PEACOCK crosses up into Saloon Stage area

PEACOCK: (*cont.*) And this blight on humanity! This sin-soaked ziggurat! Who hath sorrow? Who hath woe? They, who do not answer no! They whose feet to sin incline, while they tarry at the wine!

SADIE: What in hatchetations are you yammering about Peacock?!

PEACOCK: Yellowing? I'll say the Sheriff is yellow! It's an utter disgrace allowing you to remain in this den of impurity. Why just breathing the air in this place is bound to make one follow the way of the heathen.

SADIE: Maybe you should stop breathing for a while.

PEACOCK: I suggest you curtail your evil attitude and find another town to flaunt your wanton ways!

BILLY: The lady ain't done nuthin wrong. Why don't you leave her be?

PEACOCK: Are you addressing me, sir? (*crosses toward Billy*)

BILLY: Maybe I am and.. maybe I ain't.

PEACOCK: If you are my good man, I believe introductions are in order. I don't believe I had the pleasure.

SADIE: We know you haven't. That's why you're wound up tighter than hemp on a longhorn.

ACT ONE

PEACOCK: What are you saying? I will not stand for vile insinuations!. Especially from the likes of you.

SADIE: *(rises)* It wasn't my insinuation that was vile Peacock, it was your interpretation!

PEACOCK: Vacation? I suggest you take one yourself! Away from here!

BILLY: So I'm reckonin' this here gal can't hear worth a holler.

SADIE: Only when it suits her.

PEACOCK: Land a Goshen! Such insolence!

SADIE: While we're on the subject of insolence, *(to Billy)* this is Mrs. Peacock. Mrs. Peacock, THIS IS MR JAMES.

PEACOCK: James? Mr. James?

PEACOCK gets up close inspecting BILLY.

BILLY: And 'fore you say it, no, I ain't from around here. And no, I don't look familiar. You ain't seen me before. I'm just passin' through on my way down south.

PEACOCK: South? We'll all be on our way down south! South to Hades associating in this place!

DOC enters

DOC: Greetings and concernations to one and all.

PEACOCK: What is the meaning of this? *(crossing to Doc)*

DOC: The meaning of this? Let's see. *(speaking into her hearing horn)* Well, some say the meaning is in attaining the highest form of knowledge. From which all good and just things derive utility and value and then there's the theory of a single moral obligation..

ACT ONE

PEACOCK: Moral obligation? What are you prattling on about you dundering dolt? It's our moral obligation to set this town right! The ladies told me that ceased their right to assembly and confiscated their pitchforks! It has to start somewhere! It can start with the closing of this place!

DOC: How about we start with the closing of your mouth. We have some issues that have arisen in town and the sheriff wishes to address them.

SADIE: What kind of issues Doc?

DOC: I best leave that matter to the Sheriff.

PEACOCK: Ha! *Leave that matter to the Sheriff!?* That will get you nowhere in a hurry! I've left many a matter with the Sheriff and nothing has come of it! My garden was pillaged last night by some sneaking mis-content and do you think Sheriff Ford would do anything?

SADIE: It's probably opossum or goat.

PEACOCK: Coat? Why in heavens should I wear a coat?

SADIE: I said goat!

PEACOCK: Goat? Hasn't been a goat on my property in ages!

DOC: *(aside)* Not since Mr. Peacock departed. .

PEACOCK: What was that? *(points her horn toward Doc)*

DOC: I said *started*. Once the Sheriff gets here, we can get *started*!

BILLY: What's this 'bout Watson? What's these here *matters* the Sheriff has?

DOC: He was meeting with the Marshall about.. the matter. Essentially going over the good, the bad and the ugly of a particular situation.

ACT ONE

SHERIFF enters

DOC: (*cont.*) I'll let him tell you about the particulars of his own regard.

SHERIFF: Afternoon everyone.

PARSON GRAHAM enters

SHERIFF: Afternoon all. If I may have your attention. As you may or may not know, we were holding a particular prisoner over to the jail for a spell. This fellow was being taken to the train depot by Marshall Tucker but... last evening, our prisoner was found dead.

PEACOCK: A round head?

SADIE: Not round head, FOUND DEAD!

PEACOCK: Dead? Good riddance I say!

DOC: Dead as a doornail. He may have taken a tumble and succumbed to a blow to the head. However, I found what I believe to be a fragment of a .22 caliber bullet lodged within his left temple. Now a blow to the temple can render a man mortified but in this case, a bullet was heir apparent.

SADIE: Apparently so.

BILLY: I reckon you're talking about Sergio, is that it?

SHERIFF: You reckon rightly Billy. You wouldn't happen to know anything about this bullet would ya?

BILLY: Can't say as I do. As I showed ya yesterday, I ain't armed. Ain't carried a gun in over 5 years. 'Sides, never carried a .22. Too sloppy. Bounces too much.

SHERIFF: Would you mind tellin' me, how you happened to bounce into my town just as your old partner rides in?

ACT ONE

BILLY: Simple twist of fate. I came down from Deadwood. Was over in Ogallala for a while. Headed east. .and well, here I set. Never heard a word about my ol companero till I walked in here.

SHERIFF: Till you walked in here? And just what business do you have here in Meridosa?

BILLY: Business of chance. *(shuffles cards)* It's all I been doin' lately. Followin' my luck around the country.

SHERIFF: And by any chance, were you near the jail last night?

BILLY: Maybe I was..*(stands up from table)* and maybe I wasn't.

Moment of tension -everyone backs up expecting a fight

SHERIFF: *(approaches Billy)* Maybe you better decide. And then decide how lucky you feel right now. Cause there's a chance that maybe you are and maybe you ain't.

SADIE: And maybe I can tell you he was here most of the night playing cards with Maverick and the boys.

PEACOCK: Maybe someone should inform me why we're conducting this matter in this Benzinery! I have yet to hear one matter of importance or see what relevance any of this has! It's a disgrace!

PARSON: Mrs. Peacock, a man was killed in our town last night!

PEACOCK: That no-good outlaw? Served him right!

PARSON: Remember what is written, *Do not seek revenge or bear a grudge against anyone among your people, but love your neighbor as yourself.*

DOC: As we were saying, it appears the late Van Cleef was the victim of foul play. As to how he became a victim, well that's is a bit of a conundrum.

ACT ONE

SHERIFF: It sure is. Van Cleef was locked up tight in a cell in the back. The only way anyone could get in or out, was to come through the front.

SADIE: So did anyone come through the front door?

SHERIFF: No one while I was there. I did step out for a spell to come over here. I left Parson Graham to keep watch.

BILLY: But who will watch the watchmen? So tell us preacher, anybody come through the front?

PARSON: No, no one came through the front door... well, that is....except for...

SADIE: Except for...?

PARSON: Well, Miss Crabtree, did stop by.

BILLY: So, there ya have it, lawman. Only folks in your jail were a preacher and a teacher.

SHERIFF: Thank ya kindly Billy, but I can handle lookin' into this matter.

BILLY: Didn't mean no harm by it. Figured you could use some help in this poor excuse for a town.

SHERIFF: In this *what*? What are you sayin'?

BILLY: I'm sayin you might be the biggest toad in the puddle round here but it looks like you're a might hobbled. Ya ain't got no real deputy to lend a hand. You got nobody.

PARSON: Why that's not true! You've got the Marshall and his men to help out.

SHERIFF: (*sighs*) 'Fraid it *is* true. The Marshall and 'em is headin' back to Hadleyville.

SADIE: Heading back? You mean they left you here to sort this out by yourself? That's a lily-livered thing to do.

89

ACT ONE

DOC: You risk your skin watching criminals for people and they take the high road at the first sign of an enigma, you wind up asking questions all alone on some dirty street. For what? For nothing. For a tin star.

PEACOCK: All my born days, I've never heard of such nonsense!

SADIE: I'm surprised you can hear anything.

PEACOCK: I hear just fine you heathen!

SADIE begins speaking to Peacock but only miming words not actually saying anything.

PEACOCK: What's that? Speak up!

SADIE mimes speaking again as if she is shouting, gesturing wildly with her hands

PEACOCK: (*worried*) Great day in the morning! This blasted thing has gone foul! Can't hear a thing!

PEACOCK bangs the horn with her hand.

SHERIFF: Which brings to mind a question, did anyone *hear* anything last night? Such as a gunshot?

BILLY: Why don't 'cha ask the preacher man? He was keepin' watch.

PARSON: As I told the Sheriff, I didn't hear anything.

BILLY: And this here jail, where nobody heard nuthin', is the same place where the *shot* happened. How'd ya explain that one?

SHERIFF: Kid, I've told you once, this here's *my* business. I'll ask the questions.

SADIE: But Billy has a point! How can a man be shot with no sound and no one there to shoot him?

ACT ONE

BILLY: Who says there weren't no one there to shoot 'im? Padre was there. School marm was there. Could be she was teachin' a hard lesson. Or the preacher was introducing Sergio to his maker.

SADIE: No wonder they call you Billy *the Weasel*.

BILLY: How's that? Sounds like someone's tryin' to rustle my feelin's.

SADIE: I think you heard me! You can borrow Peacock's trumpet if you need help!

SHERIFF: That's ENOUGH!

PEACOCK: I'll say it's enough! Enough cavorting around in this gin mill. I have better things to do with my time! And I would think you would as well Sheriff! And you Parson! (*stomps off exiting*)

SADIE: Well, I guess she told us!

BILLY: Reckon she did. Seems to be another *killin* that's goin on here Sheriff - and that's the time you're killin. Should you be in here passin the time of day with us... folks who had *nuthin*' to do with nuthin? Who didn't *hear* nuthin'? Or should you be out findin somethin'?

SHERIFF: Nuthin to do with nuthin? Is that was you said? The man who was double-crossed by Van Cleef? Who spent five years in jail because of him? The man who just shows up in town right about the time Van Cleef takes a bullet? The only person who had a *reason* to give him a bullet? Ain't that somethin?

BILLY: Funny ol' world, ain't it?

SHERIFF: Yes, very funny. (*pulls gun on Billy*) Now let's see you laugh Kid! Cause now I'm arrestin' you for suspicion of murder. Now, if you'll turn around with your hands up, like they was reachin for the sky.

ACT ONE

BILLY: You're makin a big mistake. (*turns and raises hands*)

SHERIFF: Yea? Maybe I am and maybe I ain't. Get movin.

SHERIFF exits leading BILLY. . Lights down SADIE exits- Transition music -Don't Fence Me In

END OF ACT 1

ACT TWO

LIGHTS UP - JOEY is carefully (sneaking) his way up toward stage through crowd. A distance behind him is MISS CRABTREE following

MISS CRABTREE: Joey! Joey Starrett!

JOEY Freezes and turns

JOEY: Why hello Miss Crabtree! Gee! You sure look a might pretty today!

MISS CRABTREE: And where have *you* been? Why weren't you in school?

JOEY: Sorry Miss Crabtree, it's the craziest thing! You wouldn't believe me if I told ya.

MISS CRABTREE: How can I *not* believe you, if you don't tell me first?

JOEY: Well... you see... a band of Comanche swooped in last evening and I had to protect the homestead.... they was hoopin and hollarin and arrows was flyin'....

MISS CRABTREE: Joey! Stop telling such tall tales!

ACT TWO

JOEY: I told ya, you wouldn't believe me. Well, ya see .. it was... it was my stomach. I had the back door trots somethin' fierce last night and...

CRABTREE: Perhaps you'd better see Doc Watson. There he is over there. Doctor!?

JOEY: I don't need to see no dern Doctor ! The truth of the matter is... the reason my stomach is givin me fits is ... I kilt somebody!

DOC WATSON approaches

DOC: Afternoon Miss Crabtree, Joey. What seems to be the issue here?

CRABTREE: The issue is, Joseph missed his lessons today and is quite eager to create all sorts of Fiction! From a bellyache to fighting Indians and now is claiming he killed someone!

DOC: Ah yes, the follies of youth are soon to... Uh.. hang on a tick! Did you say... *killed someone?*

JOEY: Yessir. Ya see, sometimes like to pretend things. And sometimes I pretend like I'm... well, up against a mean ol gunslinger.. and we's havin' a showdown. Well sir, I was pretendin' last night and ...I went and drawed my weapon, *(pulls up hand pointing finger as if it's a gun)* ... and it went off. Sure are shootin' it did. I heard it! Then I heard that ol' Ornery eyes' turned up dead over to the jail.

CRABTREE: *(laughs)* Did you ever hear such a thing?

DOC: Actually I have! No, not that the human finger is capable of dispensing bullets, but it is true that Van Cleef was fatally wounded by a gunshot last evening.

CRABTREE: Mr. Van Cleef? Dead?

ACT TWO

DOC: Quite so. Now Joseph, tell me again about this gunshot you heard.

DOC puts arm around JOEY and they cross up toward Sheriff's office area. CRABTREE follows during dialogue below.

JOEY: Well sir, I was headed home to do my lessons. Just after I told ya I had fetched the Marshall. I reckon I was 'bout.. between the livery and home and well.... my imagination started actin' up and... got into a showdown with a fella that called me out... and well, pulled my gun and.. and there was a shot! I swear to you I heard it! Sure as I'm standin' here!

DOC: Now Joseph, if you had to tell the direction of the shot, could you tell where it came from?

CRABTREE: And please don't say from your finger.

JOEY: Well, if I was to recollect... maybe it sounded like... it came from over to my left.

DOC: To your left? From near the livery stable?

JOEY: Then again... maybe it was to my right.... or behind me somewheres. Con-sarn it! I can't recall! I got so skeered by it.. thinkin' it was me! Oh sure! I know better than to think my finger could shoot but... when I heard about Van Cleef being kilt! I ran and hid out.

JOEY sits down in chair in Sheriff's office - Sheriff walks out as scene continues

SHERIFF: Would you say the shot sounded like it came from near the jail?

JOEY: Not rightly. I was quite a ways from the jail. I would know'd a shot that came from here.

SHERIFF: And how could you tell Joey?

JOEY: Cuz when my paw goes huntin in the woods, out'n back of the house. I can pert-near tell where he is by the sound when he shoots. Kinda like when it gets to stormin'. You can tell by the thunder how fer off it is. They ain't as much echo when it's close. See Miss Crabtree, I know my science learnin !

SHERIFF: And what about you Miss Crabtree? The Parson informed me earlier that you paid a visit here.

CRABTREE: Well yes, yes I did. It may sound unorthodox, yet I saw it as an educational opportunity to be informed about.. well, current events in this town. The chance to view a true criminal behind bars. Our justice system in action.

SHERIFF: Did you have an opportunity to see or hear anything?

CRABTREE: The Parson wouldn't allow anything or *anyone* to be seen. I went straight home to prepare the following days' lesson.

DOC: And what lesson have we learned? A convicted man succumbs to bullet while no one heard a gunshot, except Joseph who stated he was quite a distance away. We've failed our math lesson because it doesn't add up.

JOEY: Maybe it was a hired gun! I hear tell - some of 'em have these German rifles with spy glasses on top. Can shoot a man from a mile away!

DOC: The bullet would have to make it through the front door, bypass the Parson and turn the corner and make back to the cell.

CRABTREE: Perhaps it came through the window.

SHERRIFF & DOC: The what?

CRABTREE: The window. In the cell. I recall asking the Parson if there was a window in the jail cell. He said there was.

ACT TWO

SHERIFF: But it's 'round back and it's about 15 feet up from the street. Ain't nobody could reach up there. Lessen they was very tall.

CRABTREE: True, is no way to peek into that window. It was just a thought.

SHERIFF: Thank ya Miss Crabtree, I will gladly take all possibilities and considerations. You and the Doc here are the most learned folks in town.

CRABTREE: Yes, unfortunately, (*clears throat*) May I ask if you are familiar with the literature of a Mr. Doyle from London England?

SHERIFF: Can't say as I am.

CRABTREE: Mr. Doyle is one to create mystery stories about a detective who solves puzzling cases. In fact, he has an associate named Doctor Watson!

DOC: No relation I assure you.

CRABTREE: Of course not Doctor, it's fiction. Anyway, being slightly familiar with these stories and the detective's methods of deducing crime, may I suggest you consider - narrowing in on a suspect, opportunity and motive first. And then follow with the method.

SHERIFF: Sure, but... I don't follow ya.

DOC: I think what she's saying is that.. we should focus on the *who*, *when* and *why*, and worry about the *how* in due time. For example, we know the *what* in this case, and that's a 22 caliber bullet.

SHERIFF: I get 'cha. The only *who* I would suspect is locked up right now. Only problem is the *when*. Far as I know, he was playin cards over at the Saloon. I'm hard pressed to think of anyone in

ACT TWO

this town who knew Onary eyes. 'Cept what what they read or heard gossip about.

CRABTREE: I'm not sure many people in this town actually read. Or even know of a world outside of Meridosa.

SHERIFF: Outside of a few folks, can't rightly point the finger at any other suspect 'cept Billy. Not even sure it's worth the effort trying to solve this matter.

DOC: The effort? *(chuckles)* What's the effort of any day, John? What's the use of getting up in the morning? You're a lawman, and you finally got a chance to do some *law*, man! Ask yourself how many mysteries on this level will test your effort? Sure you can let it wander out to pasture but do you want to lay awake at nights wondering, what if tried? What if I made the effort? What if I rounded up my resources and hauled this one in? Do you want to lie awake or do you want to sleep at night with a clear conscience?

Brief pause as Sheriff ponders what Doc said.

CRABTREE: Well, that was a highly profound and articulate outburst Doctor.

DOC: I know. I have no idea where that came from. Let's just keep it between ourselves.

SHERIFF: Doc, you're right! I guess I better start by findin' what folks in town carry a .22.

CRABTREE: If I may offer an educated opinion if most people are aware that Van Cleef was mortally wounded by this particular caliber, I doubt many will be willing to confess to owning such a weapon.

JOEY: School teacher is right! They ain't gunna tell the Sheriff!

CRABTREE: They *aren't going* to tell the Sheriff.

ACT TWO

JOEY: It's what I said Miss Crabtree. They ain't! Less they was loco or toxicated!

CRABTREE: Intoxicated, Joey. The word is intoxicated.

DOC: Exactly! Yes! You know, I may have a method whereby folks would be prone to share information, not with the Sheriff but with me. That is... a version of me in which they are accustomed. Best I start right now! *(starts to exit)*

SHERIFF: What are ya plannin' Doc?

DOC: Trust me Sheriff and just have what a Doctor has.. patience. *(exits)*

SHERIFF: Speakin of patience. Reckon I better let Billy go. Ain't much sense holdin him.

CRABTREE: Come along Joseph, we shouldn't tarry. You have some lessons to make up. Not to mention your grammar skills.

JOEY: Aw Miss Crabtree! Just when it was gettin' good!

CRABTREE and JOEY exit - SHERIFF exits

Lights down - Transition Music - Get along Little Doggies

Lights up PARSON GRAHAM is walking along street area - we suddenly hear awful singing from the voice of DOC - coming along through audience area toward Parson

DOC: *(singing)* Whoopie Ty yi yo, get along little froggies / it's your undoing so get off of the stone/ whoopsie dye doodle you stink little froggies / you know that Wyoming is no where near rome.....

PARSON: Doctor Watson? Are you all right?

DOC: *(acting overly drunk)* Who me, sir? Couldn't be butter, bitter .. uh better.

PARSON: Doc? Have you fallen?

ACT TWO

DOC: Nawwwwwww. Me? Well, yes, once while coming round the corner by the mill. Some fool left a bridal..upon the lane.

PARSON: No Doc, I meant fallen from sobriety?

DOC: Oh that that that! Yes, that. Well uh... *(takes a few steps away and motions Parson to follow)* Come 'mere come 'mere come 'mere!

PARSON: (follows) What is it?

DOC throws arm around Parson to pull in close, with other hand pulls out small silver flask from pocket - holds it up

DOC: *(drops drunken act -in sudden serious tone)* It's 100% Hydrogen with a double shot of Oxygen chaser my good man. Water. This is merely a ruse to elicit certain information. Shhh!

PARSON: Ah! I see but..

DOC: *(back to act -talking loudly pacing around)* Why yes that's correct my good man of all things spiritual and heavenly! Will no one rid me of this turbulent beast? Varmints I tell you! Taken to pilfering from the root cellar and the grain mill! Rodents the size of a chuckwagon! Need to find devices of destruction, preferably a *small caliber*. Who shall aid me in riddle... uh ..ridding me of these oppressive opossums? Anyone? *(loudly hiccups)*

PARSON: I see Doctor! I shall ask around. *(exits)*

DOC: Excellent! Excellent! A call to arms! Meet me at the Punched... Parch.... at the *saloon!* Now is the time for all good countries to come to ... the aid of... *(shrugs then takes a drink from his flask - starts to exit)*

BILLY enters

BILLY: What's all the shoutin about Watson?

ACT TWO

DOC: Shouting? (*looks around*) Who's shouting?! Be quiet I say! My friend here is trying to think! Say... I thought you were wearing striped pajamas over at the pokey!

BILLY: Sheriff decided to pull in his horns.

DOC: Did he now? Horn pulling huh? Well, swell! Welcome back to the land of freedom!

BILLY: Freedom? Well, that's just some people talkin. What's all the high falutin fuss you're makin?

DOC: Falutin fuss? Oh that! Yes, why tis a plague of varmints - come in from the fields! I'm calling for all arms to be brought with forth... with...

BILLY: Arms for what?

DOC: For.. use in... varmint removal. Looking for a hittle lelp. A little help. Assistance and such.

BILLY: Here's some assistance and such. Tell the sheriff to take a good look at the cell again. The one he kept me in. The ceilin' and the wall. Might yield some sights worth seein'. Had some time to stare at 'em. Also had time to hear people talkin'. That's right. You can drop the drunk act Doc. Ain't foolin nobody. (*exits*)

DOC: The ceiling? (*exits*)

Lights down

Lights Up -Saloon area - Sadie enters dusting off tables – STRANGER is sitting, throws down coins and exits

SHERIFF enters looking depressed reaches up removes badge and tosses it down on table

SHERIFF: Bring me a bottle and a glass Sadie.

SADIE: For a moment I thought you said *a bottle and a glass.*

ACT TWO

SHERIFF: Yep. I did.

SADIE: You want a drink?

SHERIFF: Yep.

SADIE: But aren't you....?

SHERIFF: What? Sheriff? It's what folks call me. It's what I was appointed to be. That badge there said so. Might as well take it off of me. I can't use it anymore.

SADIE picks up bottle from other table with glass and sets it down on table.

SADIE: What's the problem Sheriff?

SHERIFF: The problem is... I have been tryin' all day to get to the bottom of this here killin'. Been all over this town and ain't one person heard nor saw nuthin. I gave it a real effort Sadie. I did.

SADIE: So, now you're making an effort to get to the bottom of a bottle? It's a cheap way to run from trouble John. I know. I ran from it also. All the way here. That's the truth

SHERIFF: My truth is.. I'm ain't good at solvin' nothing. Just lecturing and lockin up drunks and finding lost cows. *(pours shot)* That I can solve. Findin' out who killed a prisoner in my jail? I ain't no count. Speakin of no count, where's Kid Vicious?

SADIE: I think you put the fear into him when you locked him up. He said he was taking his winnings and buying a horse. Heading down to New Orleans or over to St Louis.

SHERIFF: Yea? Probably what I should be doin'. I'm sure Peacock and her bunch will be asking for my resignation anytime now.

SADIE: Peacock can pester anyone into doing anything.

ACT TWO

SHERIFF: Yep. Leave it to her, she could probably find out what happened to Van Cleef.

SADIE: She probably could. Line up everyone and henpeck the dickens out of them till they fessed up.

SHERIFF: (*chuckles -takes drink*) Yea. I can see it now Sadie. She'd round 'em all up like a bunch of wild mustangs and heard 'em in.

PEACOCK enters leading PARSON, DOC, MISS CRABTREE, BILLY, JOEY enter.

SADIE: She'd have everyone presented before the town and her Ethics league..

PEACOCK: All right everyone! (*addressing Audience*) Here are they are, the lot of them! I submit to you, citizens of Meridosa and esteemed members of the Ethics Ladies Guild post 47, someone among these here, knows what happened to that malfeasant misfit Van Cleevage....

JOEY: Van Cleef.

PEACOCK: Whoever!

SHERIFF: Yep. That's just how it would sound!

SADIE: And then she'd say something like..

PEACOCK: Now if the Sheriff won't get to the bottom of this, I will! It's time for you all to answer for yourself!

DOC: Splendid notion! Here here! I second the motion issued by the lady from Peacock, now uh... what was the question?

PEACOCK: The question is, which one of you heathens broke the seventh commandment?

PARSON: Excuse me, Mrs Peacock, I believe you meant the *sixth* commandment. The seventh pertains to adultery.

PEACOCK: Idolatry? Why that's the second commandment!

ACT TWO

PARSON: Yes, I know that. I think you were speaking of murder and...

DOC: Ten of one and half dozen of another! I can speak in good faith that myself and the Sheriff were seeing to an unruly mob at the general store when said commandment was being broken. Now, that would be the one pertaining to murder. I can't speak to the one concerning adultery.

BILLY: And I was right here. Commanding a game of poker.

MISS CRABTREE: I was walking home.

JOEY: And I was ridin point on a roundup ....

MISS CRABTREE: Joseph.

JOEY: Yes ma'am. Sorry.

SADIE: (*steps in joining the imaginary scene*) And I was here, engaged in a rousing rendition of "You've Been a Good Ol' Wagon But You Broke Down"

PEACOCK: Why there is nothing at all the matter with my wagon! If I had my way, it would carry you out of town!

SADIE: And how long do you intend to carry on here Peacock?

PEACOCK: Until I get some answers little missy! (*turns to crowd*) So good citizens of Meridosa and ladies of the league, are you satisfied with the nonsense you've heard? Of course not! I put it to you fair people, would anyone like to cross-examine anyone you see? Now is your chance to make any one of them come clean! Any questions from you?

(*brief Q & A from audience - since this is in a sense an "imagined" scene between Peacock and the others - not actually based in the reality of the plot - if anyone questions Doc or Billy about what he saw on the walls or ceiling - it would be advisable to be as vague as possible.*)

ACT TWO

PEACOCK: *(to wrap up)* Well, that was a fine how do you do. I'm not for certain we got to the bottom of anything. I expected more from you people. *(can ad-lib a bit about any questions asked)*

SHERIFF: I can imagine her handling the whole thing like that.

SADIE: And better yet! I bet she would take it a step further.

SHERIFF: How so?

SADIE: *(back to scene)* What's the point of all this Peacock?

PEACOCK: The point? Why it's the American way! The democratic process! Unlike those savages.. out west in the Indian territories with no sense of decency or laws!

DOC: Yes! Send them back where they came from!

PEACOCK: We have laws and processes.

CRABTREE: Put it to a vote!

PEACOCK: Put them on a boat?

SADIE: A VOTE.

DOC: Excellent idea! Let democracy flourish I say! We elect a President. A mayor! Let's elect a murder!

PEACOCK: Marvelous idea!

DOC: It is?

PEACOCK: Let us exercise our God-given rights! *(explain voting rules to audience - if you want to include voting)*

- Characters assist in gathering votes etc... - Once votes are collected everyone will exit stage area except SHERIFF and SADIE

SHERIFF: I reckon something like that might work. Then again, they elected me. See how that worked out.

ACT TWO

SADIE: John, would you stop feeling sorry for yourself! What would happen if every time.. something didn't work out the way you wanted it? Or you ended up in a place you didn't want to be? We'd all be a bunch of crying nellies! Sorry, every minute of every day.

SHERIFF: I'm sorry but..

SADIE: But what? You want something like that to happen? You want Peacock to solve this? You want Peacock to take over as Sheriff of this town?!

SHERIFF: Why no! Of course not!

SADIE: You want to have Ethics league meetings every night and play Bridge every Sunday?

SHERIFF: I don't even know how to play bridge!

SADIE: Then you better fish or cut bait John Ford! Get on out there and save your town!

SHERIFF: *(thinks for a moment - sighs)* I'm a gettin! *(starts to exit)*

SADIE: Wait! Aren't you forgetting something? *(nods to table)*

Sheriff walks back to table looking at bottle and badge -a few beats

SADIE: Take the badge. Leave the bottle.

Picks it up and exits - lights down

LIghts UP - Peacock comes out in Street area center facing audience

PEACOCK: All right everyone! I submit to you, citizens of Meridosa and esteemed members of the Ethics Ladies Guild post 47...

SHERIFF enters

SHERIFF: Hold your horses Peacock! I can handle it from here.

PEACOCK: Of course I can hear!

ACT TWO

SHERIFF: Exactly, listen to this, citizens of Meridosa! Gather round.

DOC, PARSON, CRABTREE, JOEY, SADIE enter

SHERIFF: I learned some things about what may've happened to our prisoner over to the jail. Our esteemed Doctor Watson, was key to findin' out some things. Doc, if you will?

DOC: I will. I will also let you know

, anyone who saw me last night and concluded I had returned to my drunken vocation is sorely mistaken. It was merely *a ruse*. A charade for covert cultivations.

CRABTREE: How interesting! Just like the detective in those Doyle novels I mentioned. Wearing disguises to gather information! What did you learn Doctor?

DOC: Well, I set out to learn who amongst the townsfolk carried a particular style of firearm. One that may have put a dent in the prisoner. One thing I learned is that I should have studied the jail cell a tad closer. Specifically dents in the walls and ceiling

PARSON: What about the walls and ceiling?

SHERIFF: Well, among the usual drawin's and calendar carvin's, there was some particular scratches.. or ricochet marks . Much like a bullet would make. A bullet that came through the window.

CRABTREE: The window?

DOC: Yes, what bullet from yonder window breaks! Fortunately, Mr. Van Cleef's cranium was there to stop it, otherwise, it may have caused some real damage.

CRABTREE: Doctor really!

BILLY enters silently

ACT TWO

JOEY: A bullet through the window? Reckon some fella pulled off a trick shot like he was playin' billiards? I heard tell William Cody could shoot a silver dollar off a Buffalo's horn while he was standin' on his head inside barrell. You reckon it was a hired gun with a german rifle?

SHERIFF: No Joey. It was a small caliber. Like for small game huntin.

PARSON: So that explains the drunken ruse Doctor.

DOC: I covered the whole town. From the west side of the livery stable, down to Katie Elder's, over east - down to Marion Morrison's place. I managed to gather up a varmint vigilante group comprised of 4 rifles, 2 sling-shots and a pea shooter. None of which, was the thunder stick in we were looking for.

PARSON: Forgive me but.. I was just reminded of something. A touch of divine wisdom. If you will forgive me all for a moment. I must see about something. *(Exits quickly)*

CRABTREE: If I may ask, Sheriff you mentioned these marks.., these *ricochet* marks inside the jail cell. Doesn't that present the possibility of ...

BILLY: A bad hand? Bad luck? A bullet flyin'? A fella standin in a cell. Wrong place at the right time. Don't have to be no schoolmarm to figure that one out.

SADIE: Wrong place at the right time? Are you saying whoever shot Van Cleef may not have intended to?

SHERIFF: I ain't for certain this someone knew the consequences of their action.

JOEY: How can you not know you took down the meanest, baddest gunslinger in the area? You'd be famous! Like that there Bob Ford who shot Jesse James. Why there's songs and books 'bout him!

ACT TWO

SHERIFF: Here's the thing Joey, now ol' Jesse knew Bob Ford. Who did Sergio Van Cleef know in this town?

JOEY: Well he knew Billy! They was partners!

BILLY: I 'spect we were. For a while. Till Sergio gave me a chance to mend my villainess ways in the state pen. Sure, I had hard feelins at first. Any fella that was double-crossed would. But you get over it. Come to your senses. Come down from your fences.

PEACOCK: I thought this man was locked up!

BILLY: Maybe I was and maybe I wasn't. Maybe the Sheriff here realized - the hand he'd drawn wouldn't play.

SHERIFF: Actually, it was William Wesley here that told Doc about the marks in the cell. I guess the Kid had an ace up his sleeve. Evidence didn't support Billy as havin anything to do with it

BILLY: 'Sides. Why would I show my hand, if'n I was the one that did it? That'd be a bad deal all way 'round.

SHERIFF: Something else that struck me, if any *stranger* had a rode into town to give Onary Eyes a goin' away party, we'd know about it. Specially with Mrs. Peacock and the Ethics league keepin watch.

CRABTREE: So if it wasn't Billy and it couldn't have been a stranger...

SADIE: It was a stranger answer. Like someone who didn't know... just a stray bullet.

SHERIFF: Since the only person that said they heard anything was Joey.. and since he was near home when he heard a gunshot. It must have come from a distance from the jail. And this around the time we were scatterin' the ladies from the General Store.

ACT TWO

PEACOCK: This is all just nonsense! Spending all this time carrying on about who knows what! And you Sheriff! Should be ashamed to wear that badge! Letting criminals take room and board in this decent town, while you turn a blind eye to vagrants sneaking around my home!

DOC: Speaking of blind, once again Mrs. Peacock I see you aren't wearing your spectacles.

PEACOCK: My vegetables?! That's right! Someone has been skulking around my garden again! My tomato plants have been pilfered!

SHERIFF: This here, skulker you been talkin about, Ever get a good look at him? This peeping parker?

PEACOCK: Look at him? Why no!

PARSON: (*entering*) Have ever taken a shot at him?

PEACOCK: Take *a shot*? You know I don't touch alcohol! That's what ruined the late Mr. Peacock. Those wanton whiskey ways!

PARSON: I'm referring to your constitutional right Mrs. Peacock. Your second amendment, remember?

PEACOCK: Of course I do. Right to protect my property!

PARSON: Right. From Peeping Parkers.

SHERIFF: What is this about Parson?

PARSON: When Doc was talking about his quest to find guns, specifically the kind used for small game. I remembered the rifle Mrs. Peacock brought into the Saloon the other day. The one I took and hid inside the carriage house of the church. The one I just went to see about now. The one that is missing. But I did find a pair of spectacles. I believe these are yours, Mrs. Peacock. (*holds up pair of spectacles*)

ACT TWO

SHERIFF: Mrs. Peacock? Did you go fetch your rifle from over at the carriage house?

PEACOCK: Rifle? Why sure! I had to! That vagrant was comin each night stealing from my garden. Gettin closer. Why, even knocked upon my door one time. I had to protect myself!

SHERIFF: Did you use the rifle, Mrs Peacock? Did you shoot it?

PEACOCK: I may have! I may have leaned out the window and put the fear of God into that thief!

DOC: And you may have put a bullet into Van Cleef!

CRABTREE: You mean to say her bullet carried over to the jail? And killed Van Cleef?

SHERIFF: The angle would be 'bout right. And her homestead is over toward the Starrett place where Joey was headed.

PEACOCK: What are you saying?

SADIE: They are saying you killed Sergio Van Cleef!

PEACOCK: Why I did no such thing!

DOC: I'm afraid there's a good chance you did Peacock. Perhaps inadvertently as you were shooting at shadows out of your window, without your spectacles I could wager. I doubt you could be tried in a court of law but nonetheless... I hasten to think what you're cronies from the Ethics league are going to think!

JOEY: Why you'll be Famous Mrs. Peacock! Just like Bob Ford!

PEACOCK: Oh my lands!

PEACOCK seems faint. PARSON steadies her and consoles her. DOC, PEACOCK and PARSON speak silently as: .

ACT TWO

CRABTREE: My goodness, how exciting! I mean of course, as *a learning experience*. How the many odd pieces of information are finally weaved together into a pattern.

SHERIFF: Yep, that pattern pretty much makes a quilt that will cover this mystery now.

SADIE: What will happen to Peacock Sheriff?

SHERIFF: I'll need to bring her in to sort it out. Can't rightly charge her with no crime. I'll have to notify the Marshall about the findings. Don't see him caring much one way or the other. Peacock saved him a trip. Long tale short Sadie Mae, after this, I doubt Peacock will giving anyone much grief anymore.

SADIE: Can't say I'll miss her wrath. Well, I best be headed back. It's about time the thirsty strangers will be heading in. *(exits off singing to herself)*

DOC: Hold up Sadie Mae, I need a refill on my flask. You got anymore of that fine Sarsaparilla?

(follows her)

PARSON: Come along Mrs. Peacock, I will provide counsel. I'm sure this matter will be cleared up without too much time or worry. Remember Matthew, where it says "And who of you by being worried can add a single hour to his life?"

PEACOCK: Why it's all just ballyhoo Parson! I don't even understand what's happening!

PARSON leads PEACOCK to Exit - SHERIFF is slowly following.

JOEY: Hey Sheriff! When will you be back?

SHERIFF: Maybe tomorrow Joey. We'll have to see.

JOEY: Ya think then you can teach me how to shoot?

SHERIFF: We'll see Joey. We'll see.

ACT TWO

They exit - Joey runs off as well.

CRABTREE: *(looks to Billy)* So, you were a partner of Mr Van Cleef?

BILLY: I was.

CRABTREE: A real honest to goodness outlaw?

BILLY: Some say I was.

CRABTREE: How exciting! Are you going to be staying in town long?

BILLY: Don't reckon so. Just bought a Sorrell. Figure to be headed out town tonight. Maybe down to New Orleans or over to St. Louie.

CRABTREE: Really! Well, that sounds thrilling and adventurous!

BILLY: More thrillin' and adventurous than this town.

CRABTREE: I'll say! I'd love to have an adventure just one time in my life. *(beat)* You wouldn't by chance have room for... one more on that horse of yours would you?

BILLY: *(chuckles)* Maybe I would and maybe I wouldn't.

CRABTREE: Stay here! I'll pack my things! I'll be right back! *(runs off)*

Billy laughs - starts crossing the stage. A man enters

BILLY: Say, stranger. You're new in these parts ain't ya?

MAN: Not rightly. Used to be from these parts. Ain't been for a while. Say, that there woman they took.. .headin her over to the jail. What'd she do?

BILLY: You mean Peacock? I heard she shot a shadow just to watch him run. Why stranger? Why do you care?

ACT TWO

MAN: Well, truth of the matter is... I may've been the shadow she was shootin at.

BILLY: You? So you're the peepin parker?

MAN: Yes sir. Been out to her place every night. Didn't know how she'd take to seein' me again. Tried knocking on the door one night after I got my courage up. She'd never did answer the door. Never could hear worth yellin. Been surviving on things in her garden. Pies in the window. I thought she saw me the other night but she went and took a shot at me out the window.

BILLY: You don't say?

MAN: 'Spect I should head over there... to the jail and sort it out. *(beat)* Then again.. maybe I best... let things be. Either way, thanks for the information partner!

BILLY: Sure thing mister.

MAN: Ain't nuthin in this life is a sure thing. *(exits)*

BILLY: Adios Mr. Peacock. Adios Meridosa! *(exits)*

CRABTREE runs in with bag.

CRABTREE: Billy? *(looking around)* Billy? *(as she runs off)* Come back Billy! Billy come back!

The End

A MURDER HAS BEEN RENOUNCED
COMEDY MURDER MYSTERY PLAY

FOREWORD

A Murder Has Been Renounced was a play script that took my love of turning a cliche on its head. In this case, I used the idea of a couple traveling on a stormy night and their car breaks down. (I'm sure we have all seen that one a hundred times). They find shelter in a creepy old mansion with hopes of using a phone to call for assistance. Of course, the house is populated with some odd characters who are doing odd things. (Again -this has been done a time or two in stories and film). Throw in a stolen necklace and some gunshots, maybe a dead body, and see what develops. I brought back the characters of Nick and Darla Dashell, who are my present-day versions of Nick and Nora Charles from the Thin Man series of films. I mixed it all up with a bit of sarcasm and self awareness - threw in a curve or two and this was the result.

-Lee Mueller

PREFACE

Characters

MRS LUDOS – a very proper, no-nonsense lady of the estate of Chipping Cleghorn.

MISS HEINSPIELE – a fun-loving, gentle woman. Perhaps has a slight German accent.

CAPTAIN TRUCAGE – a boisterous gentleman. Slight shady with used car salesmen personality.

MISS MENDACIO – not the brightest bulb but loves social events none the less.

DEIDRE – the maid of the estate. Slightly sarcastic.

NICK DASHELL – private eye. Very hip and modern. Prone to make references no one understands. He does not appear smart but underneath his confused look is a very intelligent person.

DARLA DASHELL – Nick's wife. Works as a nurse and works to control Nick's wacky sense of humor.

PREFACE

Setting: Present Day – The Sitting Room of a large estate. Several large stuffed Chairs and a couch. A doorway Upstage right leads out to the hallway. A character exiting the doorway goes to the right to the front door and to the left leads off to the stairway.

A doorway upstage left leads off to the kitchen.

Set ideas – the upstage wall can contain a fireplace mantel and bookcase on either side. Perhaps a few paintings adorn the other walls.

Notes on punctuation

A slash (/) indicates a point of interruption in dialogue by an actor with the next line. The following line should begin immediately as an overlap of the previous actor's line.

Ellipses .... represent a loss of thought or words at the end of a line

ACT I

Lights up

MRS LUDOS, MISS HEINSPIELE, CAPTAIN TRUCAGE and MISS MENDACIO enter laughing as if in mid-conversation. Ludos and Trucage are holding papers. Miss Heinspiele is holding a few 8x5 cards. Mendacio is holding a folded newspaper. The first few lines are spoken normally, that is in the plain voice of the actor as they continue they develop fake British or proper British accents.

LUDOS: And so, everyone knows what to do, correct?

HEINSPIELE: Yes, but.. *(looks around)* Are we all here?

TRUCAGE: Well, I'm here!

HEINSPIELE: Yes, I know *you're* here! I mean, *all* who were invited. We seem a bit short!

TRUCAGE: Well.. we all seem shorter in person. *(laughs at his own joke)*

LUDOS: *(starts accent)* Captain Trucage! Please! Miss Heinspiele is, of course, referring to our attendance, not our altitude!

HEINSPIELE: According to this, (*looks at paper*) there should be more!

MENDACIO: (*starts accent*) Perhaps more will be here. The weather is a bit much this evening.

DEIDRE enters with a tray containing a few drinking glasses.

DEIDRE: There's trouble at mill.

LUDOS: There's trouble at what? (*takes a glass from tray*)

TRUCAGE: What mill? (*takes a glass from tray*)

DEIDRE: It's just an expression. What I mean to say is that I'm afraid the weather has interfered. Not to mention the roads and phone lines.

HEINSPIELE: The roads and phone lines? (*takes a glass from tray*)

MENDACIO: She said not to mention them.

DEIDRE: Again, it's just an expression. Mary Westmacott called to say Hillcrest road has washed out and they had to turn around. She began to express her apologies and the line went dead.

LUDOS: How unfortunate. Anyway, we'd better get on with it.

TRUCAGE: Indeed we should.

MEDACIO: Oh yes. It should be fun! (*takes a glass from tray lays newspaper down on table*)

LUDOS: If the rest make it here, they will assimilate.

HEINSPIELE: Shall we?

LUDOS, HEINSPIELE, TRUCAGE, MEDACIO lift glasses as toast

TRUCAGE: Once more unto the breach dear friends! Once more!

They drink - each set glasses down various places, table, book shelf etc and cross up right to hallway -

LUDOS: La chasse est ouverte!

SOUND CUE *Thunder*

DEIDRE turns and exits off left doorway We Hear Knocking on a door (right)

SOUND CUE *Thunder again and* LIGHTS *flicker*

We Hear knocking again – a bit more forceful - A pause -then we hear

DARLA: *(calling out off stage)* Hello? Anyone home?

NICK: *(off)* Hello?!

DARLA: *(off)* Hello?

NICK: *(off)* Hola? *(beat)* Bon-jour? *(beat)* Guten-tag?!

DARLA: *(off)* Seriously?

NICK and DARLA DASHALL peek into the room from the right side of hallway archway.

NICK: Anyone? Bueler? Bueler?

DARLA: Stop it, Nick.

NICK: *(pointing off to left)* Maybe they're upstairs.

They enter wet from the rain. Both are wearing coats. NICK stamps feet shakes umbrella. He is wearing a Deerstalker style hat –they look around the room.

DARLA: There's no one in here. *(looking at empty glasses)* But there was! Looks like there was a celebration recently.

NICK: *(picks up empty glass)* And it's still warm!

DARLA: *(sighs at Nick)* At least it's warm in here.

NICK: So, what are the rules for wandering into someone's home unannounced? Do you go looking and find them or just kinda hang until they find you.

DARLA: Let's just remain here and find out.

NICK: All those in favor say aye or I. Because *I* certainly am not going back outside! It's wretched out there. And wet too! (*removes hat shaking it to dry it off*)

DARLA: At least the lights are on so..and who just leaves the door open?

NICK: Well, people in this neck of the upper echelon do all sorts of wacky things. They can afford to!

DARLA: (*checking her cellphone*) But they can't afford a decent cell tower! Still no signal!

NICK: Maybe they can afford us a little accommodation. Like a phone. Like real one with wires and stuff that plug into the wall.

DARLA: Seriously Nick! Look at us! Would you let people dressed like us, use the phone?

DEIDRE enters from doorway left holding a candle in a candlestick and tray under his arm.

DEIDRE: Oh hello! You've made it!

NICK: We did?

DARLA: No! We're not..

NICK: (*interrupting*) Yes! Yes, we did! Make it that is! Weather's not fit for man nor fowl!

DEIDRE: I'm sorry sir? (*setting candlestick down*)

NICK: Why? It's not your fault it's raining.

DEIDRE: No sir. I meant, *sorry* as in.. I did not hear what sir was saying.

DEIDRE continues on gathering up empty glasses on her tray

DARLA: Uhh..Sir was saying the weather is quite foul.

NICK: No, Darla. I said the weather's not fit for man nor fowl. Fowl as in..you know.. bird. I was going for a pun.

DEIDRE: Yes, most hilarious I'm sure. Pardon me, but I take it this is part of the....milieu?

NICK: The mill what?

DEIDRE: No. Part of the whole... .you know. *(sighs)* Very good. I'll play along. *(clears throat)* May I be of some service?

NICK: Service? Yea, that would be awesome! Because our phones have no service out in this neck of the woods.

DEIDRE: Yes, we are rather remote here at the Chipping Cleghorn estate. Communications are an issue.

NICK: So are you the... maid? No offense, I'm just assuming, I mean you're dressed like what I'd imagine a maid would be dressed like. With the whole maid like look... and the tray with the whole tidying up maidy thing.

DEIDRE: Uh.. yes. Sure. The maid. My name is Deidre.

NICK: Deidre? Of course, it is. I mean it's very maid-esqe. It always Deidre, Helga or Mitzi or something exotic.

DARLA: Actually Deidre, the fact is, we're not ... what I mean is, we sort of.. just walked in. We tried the doorbell and it didn't seem to be working and then we tried knocking and well, forgive us... I apologize! We're Nick and Darla Dashall. We ran into some trouble a ways back down the road.

NICK: Maybe like a clogged fuel line, or fuel pump, fuel filter... you know something fuel-related... where fuel is not getting to the.. fuel thing. Any-who, saw the lights on here and well, here we are..

DARLA: Two soaking wet strangers dripping all over your floor.

DEIDRE: I see. The stranded travelers. Very good. Nice variation. May I take your coats? (*sets tray with glasses down*)

DARLA: (*confused*) Variation?

NICK: Absolutely! Thanks!

NICK removes the coat and is wearing a "Sherlock Holmes" style costume with Houndstooth Coat With attached cape hand it over to DEIDRE. DARLA removes her coat and has a nurse's uniform with several splatters of fake blood on it and her white nylons have several rips.

DEIDRE: (to *Nick*) Very fitting costume might I say.

NICK: Of course you can say! (*Nick puts back on the Deerstalker cap*) But can you guess?

DEIDRE: I believe I can. It's elementary! No offense, I'm just assuming, I mean you're dressed like what I'd imagine...

NICK: Spot on Deeds! That's correct! (*beat*) Victorian Vampire! I had some fangs... (*searches pockets*) .. I think I dropped them somewhere along the way. But anyway, my dear wife Darla here is the classic B-movie Zombie Nurse! Or I should say *was*. (*looking at Darla's face*) It looks like the rain sort of created a buzz kill.

DARLA: Anyway Deidre, do you think we could use your phone, we won't be any bother.

DEIDRE: Phone? I'm sorry but the phone service is a tad spotty. The lines may bee down due to the weather. From what I'm lead to believe some of the roads are impassible as well.

NICK: Impassible roads and impossible phones? Are you sure?

DEIDRE: Quite sure sir. What I am not sure about are the lights. The power in the area has been fluctuating and lights have been flickering. I've gathered candles in case.

NICK: Wow bummer. Hey, do you think I might wash my hands somewhere? They're a bit greasy and oily and fuely... in case we have to use the candles. I don't want to.. combust or anything.

DARLA: And maybe try the phone again. Just in case.

DEIDRE: Sure, we can try. If you would like to follow me.

DEIDRE begins to cross Stage Left Door to exit

NICK: Thanks Dee! Be right with you! (*starts to cross stops and turns to Darla*) Darla, yea I know this is a bit of a drag, you know with the car and rain and all..

DARLA: Just a "bit" of a drag Nick? No, this is off the scale! You talk me into going to some nerd fest Costume party. But we're stuck in the middle of nowhere! I could be home, warm and dry. Watching TV or reading a book. But I'm not. I'm cold and wet standing in a strange place dressed in a strange costume!

NICK: Darla, please. More sunshine! Less flippancy! (*exits*)

DARLA: (*yelling after him*) Zombies are supposed to be flippant Nick! (*quieter to herself*) There is no sunshine for the walking dead health care workers! Flippancy ensues. I mean who wouldn't be a tad flippant in this situation? (*beat*) Are you talking to yourself, Darla? Why yes. Yes, I am! (*wanders around room looking*) It's raining buckets outside and we stumble into a big old creepy house. The lines are down. Roads are washed out. A maid named Deidre. We've walked into a bad cliché! The one that begins with the line, It was a dark and stormy night. (beat) Tonight! On a very special episode of *Suspense Mystery theatre*. (*notices newspaper on table. Picks it up, sits down on couch*) Cue Miss Marple!

DARLA opens paper to read. Headline on front in big letters "Crazed Killer On The Loose"

MRS LUDOS and MISS MENDACIO enter from hallway up right – DARLA remains still hiding behind paper – Ludos and Mendacino speaking with British accents (not necessarily good accents)

LUDOS: (*as she is entering*) And I said, Miss Haversham, you know I always take my tea black with two sugars. I don't know why you believe I have always taken it white.

MENDACIO: Speaking of tea, I just read somewhere, that they have found her body.

LUDOS: Where?

MENDACIO: It was in the newspaper.

DARLA peaks from behind newspaper around to read headline, Looks shocked.

LUDOS: No, dear, I mean "where" did they find her body?

MENDACIO: I'm not sure. Some here. Some there. In several places.

LUDOS: That's her all over. Poor Miss Haversham. You know, I have also heard that Captain Trucage was the last person to see her alive. In one piece that is.

MENDACIO: Hopefully he won't be the last to see us alive! I do find him rather.. mysterious.

LUDOS: Oh yes as do I. Under his seemingly harmless appearance and manner, there could be an evil perpetrator lurking. I would not want to be left alone with him!

MENDACIO: Yes! I do hope the others will make it here this evening!

DARLA stands up

A MURDER HAS BEEN RENOUNCED

MENDACIO: *(noticing Darla)* Oh splendid! Nurse Christie! You've made it!

DARLA: Who? Yes, but no, I'm not... *(begins to cross toward Ludos)*

MENDACIO: Mrs. Ludos! It just occurred to me!

DARLA: ..actually.. my husband and I..

LUDOS: Heavens yes! We left poor Miss Heinspiele alone upstairs with Captain Trucage! What were we thinking!

MENDACIO: Tea! We were thinking about tea!

DARLA: Hello? Excuse (/) me but...

LUDOS: We must go at once!

MRS LUDOS and MISS MENDACIO run off to hallway up right

DARLA:*(continuing only to herself)* ..I'm not .. whoever... whatever! *(short pause)* Are you talking to yourself again Darla?

NICK enters from doorway left wiping off his hands with a towel

NICK: Who are you talking to Darla?

DARLA: Yes, exactly!

NICK: I'm sorry, did I miss something?

DARLA: Yes! You missed quite a lot! Like the two weird tea ladies and the mutilated body.

NICK: What? *(looks around)* I was only gone for a few minutes!! What happened?

DARLA: Some ladies came in here talking about tea and something about some woman... Miss Haversham. They found her all over. And then they saw me and called me Nurse Chrissy or somebody! And suddenly they realized they left someone alone upstairs with the guy. Look at this! *(hands him newspaper)*

NICK: What is this?

DARLA: It's called a *newspaper*. It's what people used to get news and information from before the inter-webs!

NICK: *(looks at the paper -reading out loud)* "Crazed killer on the loose. In or about the area of Chipping Cleghorn...

DARLA: Yea, I've heard that name somewhere.

NICK: I've heard the name Foghorn Leghorn! But he's a big rooster. Wait a tick! Cleghorn? Didn't Deidre mention that? As in, that was the name of this area?

DARLA: Yes I think she did, but I know that name from something else.

NICK: Anyway. *(reading)* "A string of homicides are believed to be the act of one individual whose identity and whereabouts remain unknown. So be on the lookout!" *(beat) On the lookout* for what? Who writes this stuff?

DARLA: The tea ladies were saying something about..who was it? Mr...Trucage? He was the last person to see this Haversham person. And that this Heins..spill was alone upstairs with him. And they panicked and ran off.

NICK: Who ran off?

DARLA: And it's odd that one of the ladies acted as if she knew me!

NICK: Who knew you?

DARLA: One of the Tea ladies! Aren't you listening?

NICK: I'm trying! Somebody was the last person to see somebody (/) and then...

DARLA: No! Listen! This Trucage .. was the last person to see this Haversham lady. Suddenly they realized he was alone with this Heins lady and they ran off!

NICK: OK. Let's try this again. (*beat*) *Who* ran off?

DARLA: The tea ladies!

NICK: (*beat*) So, where does the "tea" come into play?

DARLA: Nowhere! Forget the tea! They were saying Haversham was found in pieces after seeing this Trucage and they left someone alone with (/) him and..

NICK: I know! "They ran off!" I remember that part. Where did they run off to?

DARLA: (*points*) Upstairs I guess! I don't know. Maybe we should get out of this crazy place and just wait in the car.

NICK: Or maybe we should do something!

DARLA: Do something? Do what?

NICK: What else can we do? We can't go anywhere! It's a torrential downpour! The cell signal doesn't work! The regular phone doesn't work! The car doesn't work! But me? I work! I should do what I do best!

DARLA: That's what I was afraid of! You want to play a detective!

NICK: No, I'm a Victorian Vampire!

DARLA: No Nick dear! Not tonight! I'm talking *real* life!

The lights flicker off and then back on. A scream is heard off stage in the distance

NICK: Right! And that sounded like a *real* scream! Time for me to run off!

NICK runs off to hallway up right –

DARLA: *(as he is running)* But Nick! Maybe we should wait to (/) find out if....

NICK: No time for this! I need to find out about that! *(NICK exits)*

DARLA: *(sighs)* OK Yea. Find out, Nick. Find out if maybe *this* is the house on haunted hill. *(crosses back looking around)* Maybe some eccentric rich lunatic invited everyone here tonight and will pay out a fortune to whoever spends the night. And lives. And then 13 ghosts will appear. *(crosses over toward left doorway)* Or maybe this is the one where we're on Elm street or this is the home of Mother Bates and the crazed Killer is actually..

DEIDRE enters quickly through Left Doorway holding a large knife – there is blood on her hand

DARLA: Ah! *(very startled)* OH! Deidre! You scared the life out of me!

DEIDRE: Every so sorry ma'am. Not my intention. I thought I heard someone speaking and I thought the others were in here.

DARLA: Others? *(looks around)* No. No others. Earlier, yes, there were others, but now... just me. Again. By myself. Talking that is. To my...*(noticing blood on DEIDRE hand)* ..self. *(nervous)* Is that uh... blood by chance?

DEIDRE: Yes, a very good chance indeed. I was preparing some slices and when the lights went out, I slipped and nicked the dickens out of my finger.

DARLA: *(relaxes)* Oh my. Let me take a look at it!

DARLA reaches out for his hand, DEIDRE pulls back a little hesitant.

DARLA: Don't worry. I really do have a medical background. Seriously. *(she takes his hand to look at it)* This was my husband's idea for a costume. (*examines his hand*) Yea, that's a nasty cut there. We should run some cold water on it. Clean it up. Do you have gauze or band-aids?

DEIDRE: Yes, of course. Out in the kitchen. Right this way. (*starts to exit out left doorway*)

DARLA: (*follows then stops*) Oh wait! My husband! We heard a scream and (/) he went..

DEIDRE: Did you say scream?

DARLA: Yes. And my husband went to investigate. You see, in real life, my husband is a...

MISS HEINSPIELE suddenly enters from Left Doorway

HEINSPIELE: OH! Deidre! There you are! We were just upstairs wondering when the treats and light refreshments would be ready?

DEIDRE: I was working on it.

HEINSPIELE: We were also wondering if anyone else made it. (*looking at Darla*) Oh good! You're here! Love the costume!

DARLA: Yes, I'm .. uh..here. Did you say *Heinspiele*?

HEINSPIELE: Yes! Ever so glad to meet you, dear. (*back to DEIDRE*) What should I tell them? An hour or so?

DEIDRE: Yes. That would be sufficient. I should have everything ready.

HEINSPIELE: Wonderful! I'll go back upstairs and let them know! (*to Darla*) So glad you could make it. Frightful weather!

HEINSPIELE cross and exits up hallway exits to left.

DARLA: (*as Heinspiele crosses*) Yes.. it's very frightful. (*to DEIDRE*) I guess she's not in that much danger

DEIDRE: Only some of the time. (*beat*) Shall we tend to the matter at hand? (*lifts bloody hand*)

DARLA: (*sighs*) Sure! Why not!

DEIDRE and DARLA exit out Left door.

SOUND: Thunder. LIGHTS flicker

TRUCAGE silently enters through RIGHT doorway. He looks around to make sure no one sees or hears him. He crosses over to Left Door and listens for a moment. He crosses back to center and reaches in the jacket pocket and removes necklace – looking closely at and smiles. As he speaks he does so very broadly and dramatically as if performing

TRUCAGE: Keep me out the loop will you! Ha! I'll show you how to win this venture! Nothing but a stage? Maybe. But in this stage of the event, I know my exits and entrances and can play many parts. And win many a tourney!

SOUND: Knock at front door (off)

TRUCAGE looks around nervously. Starts to put jewelry back in pocket but stops. Quickly crosses over to couch, lifts cushion and hides necklaces under it.

At this moment DARLA peers out from doorway LEFT

DARLA: (*speaking back as if to DEIDRE*) No, It sounded as if it were coming from out here and.. (*seeing Trucage*) Oh! Hello!

TRUCAGE: Hellooooo nurse!

DARLA: I thought I heard someone.

TRUCAGE: Someone? Yes! That someone would be me. (*crossing to Darla*) And to who do I have the pleasure?

DARLA: Well, the pleasure would be telling you I'm.. *Mrs.* Dashell. Mrs. Darla Dashall.

TRUCAGE: Is that so? A Mrs.? Such a shame!

DARLA: Probably. And you are?

TRUCAGE: Captain Montgomery Trucage! You may call me Monty.

DARLA: Ah! Yes, I've heard *about* you.

TRUCAGE: You have? Splendid! Splendid! But you have me at a disadvantage dear Darla, I know nothing of you! Tsk tsk that I should stand here and wonder? Prey let us solve one mystery, shall we?

DARLA: One mystery would be.. why are you talking that way?

TRUCAGE: And how do you wish me to speak?

DARLA: Maybe a little more present day, a little less Jane Austen.

TRUCAGE: Very good Darla! And what is your role this evening?

DARLA: My role? Well, I thought it would be obvious by my appearance. (*beat*) Tax accountant.

SOUND: *Knock at front door (off)*

TRUCAGE: Ah! Yes. Speaking of taxing, I should get the door! Won't be a moment.

Turns crosses to up right hallway –

TRUCAGE: Yes! Yes! Coming! (*exits to right off stage*)

DARLA turns and crosses to Left Doorway as if to exit – but hesitates to listen as:

TRUCAGE: (*off*) Hello! Welcome! (*beat*) Oh! It's you!

Two quick gunshots (off) interrupt. Darla reacts in horror not sure what to do.

DEIDRE enters from doorway left. Her hand is wrapped in dish towel.

DEIDRE: Is someone knocking at the door?

DARLA points toward upstage Right doorway -crossing to DEIDRE

DARLA: No! No knocking. (*waves hands gesturing to be quiet – then whispering loudly pointing*) Shots! Gunshots! Out there! Shhhh!

DEIDRE: Shots? (*begins to cross up right*)

DARLA: (*stops DEIDRE -still whispering*) At the door! There's someone with a gun! I think they shot Trucage!

DEIDRE: But *gun*shots? That wasn't.. hmm. Interesting.

DARLA: I need to find my husband!

DEIDRE: Where is he?

DARLA: He went to see about the scream!

DEIDRE: Ah yes! The scream.

DARLA: Now he needs to see about the shots.

DEIDRE: Yes. The shots. (*calmly crosses to exit out Door left*)

DARLA: Wait! (*whispering loudly*) Where are you going? Someone may have been shot!

DEIDRE: You're a nurse. *You* see to the victim, I must see to the vegetables. (*exits*)

DARLA turns slowly and takes a few steps toward up right doorway.

DARLA: Seriously? (*beat*) Right! I should probably go and check... (*takes a few steps and stops*) But.. wait! What if they're still out there... with a gun. (*beat -goes and picks up candlestick – removes candle and tosses it*) OK! (*loudly*) I have a candlestick and I'm not afraid to use it! (*takes a few more steps – to herself*) If there's someone there, they're being awfully quiet. Maybe they left? Ran away? How do you know? I don't. You really should go and see. OK, I will.

Darla takes quiet steps, sneaking toward up right doorway. Just as she reaches doorway and begins to peak around raising candle stick– NICK enters suddenly -they startle each other

DARLA: NICK!!

NICK: DARLA!!

DARLA grabs him and pulls him away from doorway

DARLA: *(whispering loudly)* There's someone with a gun!

NICK: *(whispering loudly)* Gun? Where?

DARLA: *(whispering loudly)* Out there!! At the door!!

Nick steps back and looks out doorway toward right.

NICK: *(speaks normal volume)* Out there? There's no one at the door.

DARLA: What about the body!?

NICK: The body? *(looks around left and right)* What body?

DARLA: What? *(Crosses and looks out doorway)* The body of the guy that was shot! They shot him!

NICK: Shot who?

DARLA: Trucage! *(crosses back into room)*

NICK: Why does all this stuff happen when I leave?! *(crosses to Darla)*

DARLA: He was just in here! I saw him *here* in this room. We spoke and someone knocked...at the door. He went out there to answer it. He said something to.. and then gunshots.!!

NICK. Hang on. Rewind! You're sure it was Trucage you saw?

DARLA: Yes! He told me his name. We talked for a minute. He was quite smarmy.

NICK: So I've heard.

DARLA: Didn't you *hear* the shots?

NICK: I heard something. Maybe it was the shots, maybe the knocking.

DARLA: What about the scream?

NICK: One of your "tea" ladies lost something. A necklace or something. She screamed. You know how you girls are with your accessories. What's with the candlestick?

DARLA: It's an accessory. Protection. From people with guns. Who knock at the door. And shoot people.

NICK: So where are these people? The people with guns?

DARLA: I don't know. You're the detective. You tell me!

NICK: Good answer. Or... question. Whatever the case may be.

DARLA: So what is the case?

NICK: Well, the case of the disappearing necklace... and...

DARLA: ..disappearing shooter and shootie.

NICK: Shall we start looking?

DARLA: After you.

NICK: Me? Ladies first. Ladies with candlesticks that is.

DARLA gives him a look

NICK: All right! Very well.

NICK exits right follow by Darla

Lights down.

A MURDER HAS BEEN RENOUNCED

LIGHTS UP - MRS LUDOS, MISS HEINSPIELE and MISS MENDACIO are seated sipping from teacups. They continue speaking with faux British accents except where noted.

LUDOS: But I don't understand! Where could he have gotten to?

HEINSPIELE: Well, he was there one moment and the next.. not! Very strange!

MENDACIO: Most strange indeed. I should say! *(beat)* I should also ask, who are we talking about? Captain Trucage or that strange detective like person?

HEINSPIELE: Well, I suppose both at this point.

LUDOS: Yes, and more to the point, where did this strange detective person come from?

MENDACIO: He came because of your scream I believe.

LUDOS: *(drops accent for this line)* No, I mean for the evening's festivities. I don't recall a detective. *(beat)* Yet.

HEINSPIELE: But I'm thankful he is here..or was. That nasty business with the necklace

MENDACIO: Where could it have gotten to?

LUDOS: More like.. who could have gotten to it!

HEINSPIELE: Maybe this detective fellow will find your necklace. Awfully convenient if you ask me! Necklace disappears and a strange detective appears!

DEIDRE enters

HEINSPIELE: Oh Deidre, we were just wondering, have you seen our gentlemen?

DEIDRE: Your gentlemen?

LUDOS: She means the fellow parading as a detective.

DEIDRE: Oh him. Actually, he prefers "Victorian" vampire.

MENDACIO: Vampire?

DEIDRE: I believe he went to investigate the scream.

HEINSPIELE: The scream?

DEIDRE: And his wife, the zombie, went to investigate the gunshots.

LUDOS: (*no accent*) Gunshots?

MENDACIO: Zombie?

DEIDRE: She is a nurse in real life. Said she was. Bandaged up my hand.

HEINSPIELE: Ah! That would be Nurse Christy!

LUDOS: (*no accent*) What gunshots?

DEIDRE: The gunshots from the doorway.

HEINSPIELE: You remember Nurse Christie don't you dear? We met earlier.

LUDOS: (*resumes accent*) What of these gunshots? Who was shot?

DEIDRE: I believe Darla was under the assumption that Captain Trucage may have been involved somehow. Perhaps being the recipient of said shots. She went to see.

MENDACIO: I don't recall zombies being a part of the evening. How entertaining! This adds to the evening, doesn't it?

LUDOS: How Miss Mendacio?! How does this add to the evening?

MENDACIO: Well, first your necklace turns ups missing and then the detective appears from nowhere. And now gunshots!

HEINSPIELE: I guess she has a point. It notches it up from the standard fare we're accustomed to.

LUDOS: That it does, but it's just that... it's progressing rather quickly! We have had treats and light refreshments yet.

HEINSPIELE: Who cares? I for one grow tired of the same old thing. Our annual gatherings have become.. predictable! I vote we continue! Who knows what other frivolities may occur? I mean, here we were worried about the evening, the weather and everyone canceling!

MENDACIO: Now we have gunshots, vampires and zombies. Oh my!

HEINSPIELE: Perhaps it's like they say, less is more! Speaking of more, you know dearies, it's just about the Red Hour!

DEIDRE: Shall I get the light refreshments before anything else happens? *(begins to cross to exit)*

HEINSPIELE: Thank you, Deidre, you've been an absolute dear this evening. Allow me to see to it! *(crosses to exit off left)* I brought some ladyfingers this evening, I'll just pop in and see to them!

(Heinspiele exits and Deidre remains THE LIGHTS BLINK)

LUDOS: Great! That's all we need now is for the lights to go out.

MENDACIO: It would be fitting though don't you think Miss Ludos?

LUDOS: It could be! Especially during that dreadful musical convocation.

MENDACIO: You mean The Red Hour?

LUDOS: Do stop referring to it as such. You know I abhor obscure references!

DEIDRE: Shall I do the honors, ma'am?

LUDOS: Sure. Why not. Let's get this bloody thing going.

MENDACIO: Shouldn't we wait for Mrs. Heinspiele? She does so enjoy it!

LUDOS: And since I do not enjoy it, I will go and tell her. You may continue.

LUDOS crosses and exits left

DEIDRE walks over and turns on a music player – CD or iPod – old cheezy 60's instrumental dance music comes on as music begins – DEIDRE remains upstage watching. MRS MENDACIO spins with an interpretive style dance.

MISS LUDOS re-enters and paces around not wanting to participate. This goes on for a while – NICK and DARLA enter from RIGHT and stand for a moment somewhat amused at the scene. NICK relents and begins his own little interpretive dance, DARLA tries to stop him. MRS LUDOS finally sees Nick and Darla and waves furiously to DEIDRE to turn off the music. MUSIC STOPS.

NICK: Well, don't stop on our account! Party people in the house! La dee da dee, we like to party, We don't cause trouble, we don't bother nobody!

DARLA: Nick! Please! Stop!

MENDACIO: We weren't supposed to stop! Not yet! It's the red hour!

NICK: Red hour? Like from episode 21 of Star Trek?

DEIDRE: Unfortunately. It's all part of the evening. The festivities! You know.

NICK: Oh I get ya. The festivities. A little chance to bust a move. Watch each other whip and nae nae. I'm hip.

LUDOS: Mr. Detective! We were wondering where in the world you got to!

NICK: Me? Well, I *got to* look all over the place! High and low for the signs of any shooting or anybody.. that is as in any*body*, not just anybody... but an actual, you know, body.

MENDACIO: Did you find the necklace?

NICK: Necklace? Uh... no, not as such. Because I was thinking, instead of the necklace, I'd look into the alleged shooting and possible homicide. Maybe it's me but...

LUDOS: No, no. I apologize for Mrs. Mendacio by all means, you should look into the *shooting* first and foremost! I would say that is important, wouldn't you Mrs. Mendacio?

MENDACIO: Oh yes! Yes indeed! Shooting. Yes.

NICK: That's not to say, I couldn't look for the necklace as well. I'm not having much luck finding anyone with bullet holes.

DARLA: Speaking of which, have you ladies seen Captain Trucage by chance?

MENDACIO: Why yes! Of course, I have seen him. On several occasions!

LUDOS: I believe she is referring to an occasion that would exist in the realm of very recently.

DARLA: Such as the last 30 minutes or so..realm.

LUDOS: I believe I can help. Captain Trucage was upstairs with us earlier in the evening. The "us" would be myself, Miss Mendacio and Mrs. Heinspiele. We were all admiring the new portrait in the west hallway. Then I believe we retired to our respective rooms to freshen up. Miss Mendacio and I came down here.. where we met you, *(indicates Darla)* and we have not seen him since.

DARLA: And Mrs. Heinspiele? Where is she?

MENDACIO: She went out to the kitchen to get her fingers.

NICK: Oh. Are they missing too?

MENDACIO: Oh I hope not! *(walks upstage with back to audience as if checking something)*

DARLA: Nick really! Can't you be serious for one minute? There's something weird going on in this place.

NICK: I am being serious. And seriously, we must consider the fact that *you* dear were the last person to see Trucage! Alive or otherwise. I consider that weird! Not to mention, your tale of the gunshots!

DARLA: Nick I am telling you it happened just like I said. I came out of the kitchen because I heard someone talking, it was Trucage. Someone knocked on the front door! *(she crosses right toward doorway)* He walked out there, opened the door... I heard him say something like "*Oh it's you.*" Which is exactly what every victim says when they answer a door!

NICK: And then?

DARLA: And then gunshots!

NICK: And then?

DARLA: And then Deidre came out of the kitchen.

DEIDRE: That's right. Speaking of the kitchen, I should get back out there and see if she's found her fingers. *(crosses and exits)*

LUDOS: Oh yea please do! Who knows who else or what else will turn up missing!

DEIDRE crosses and exits – MENDACIO turns back and crosses down to group

NICK: So, to make sure I am not missing anything, you heard a voice. You came from the kitchen out here into the ..the ..whatever this room is... what is this room by the way.. Living room? Drawing Room? Parlor?

LUDOS: We refer to it as the sitting room.

NICK: Sitting? I stand corrected. Anyway, you say you saw Captain Trucage in here. You spoke to him. "Hello, how are you?" "I am fine." "Blah blah blah". Suddenly, there's was a knock at the door.

We Hear a KNOCK on the door (off stage)

NICK: *(cont.)* Probably like that! *(walks over to doorway)* Trucage walks over and goes out to answer it.

NICK exits as if to answer door.

DARLA: *(alarmed)* Nick wait! *(quickly cross to stop him)*

THE LIGHTS Go out.

LUDOS: I had a feeling that would happen! It's probably the breakers out in the kitchen. Bad weather always trips them. A little water here, some little wires there. Darkness ensues.

MENDACIO: Shall I go see about the breakers? Out in the kitchen? I can take care of it.

LUDOS: If you can manage! There's a utility box on the south wall. Miss Heinspiele can help you.

MENDACIO: No problem. I'll take care go take care of it.

MENDACIO feels her way out exiting

DARLA: Nick? (beat) Nick! Are you all right?

NICK: (*offstage*) I think so. Having a bit of an issue seeing at the moment.

DARLA: Who's at the door?

NICK: (*off*) Who's on the floor?

DARLA: No Nick! I said the door!

NICK: Yes. Yes, I am at the door. I'm trying to find the handle. (*beat*) I think I have it! Yes! (*beat*) No, wait! This is not a door. It's the hall tree. I found our coats if we need them.

DARLA: I'll file that under fun fact.

NICK: If whoever is knocking, if you could knock again?

(*A few more knocks*)

NICK: Brilliant. That helps. (*beat*) Ah! I think found something handle-ish. Might be it. Maybe not.

DARLA: Don't you have your flashlight?

NICK: Flashlight?

DARLA: Yes. You always carry it.

NICK: I do? (*beat*) Oh! Right! I do! Searching the pockets now. (*beat*) Not that one. Wait! I think.. no. That's a pen. And my car keys. Found some mints. Where did I get mints?

DARLA: Nick! Forget the mints.

NICK: Right! Mints forgotten! Wait! What's this? Ha! Score! Let there be light! I see the door! Opening now! The eagle has landed. (*beat*) Oh! It's you!

DARLA: (*waits a few beats*) Nick? Who's at the door Nick?!

NICK: Do you mean, besides me?

DARLA: Yes!

A MURDER HAS BEEN RENOUNCED

The LIGHTS come back up

LUDOS: Miss Mendacio must have found the target.

DARLA crosses toward the doorway. She stops suddenly and slowly begins backing up into the room. MR TRUCAGE enters -he appears disheveled. There is a gag (handkerchief) around his mouth and his hands are bound together in front. LUDOS and slightly -gasp etc... NICK assists TRUCAGE by removing gag -which comes off quite easily.

TRUCAGE: Thanks ever so much old boy! Bit of a sticky wicket, if I do say!

LUDOS: Captain Trucage! What on earth happened?

TRUCAGE: Not sure! There was a knock at (/) the door..

NICK: We know. We've seen this bit a few times now.

TRUCAGE: (*confused*) I'm sorry? Seen what bit?

DARLA: Never mind Captain, we all know about the knock at the door. Please tell us what happened next. Like *who* was at the door when you answered it.

MENDACIO enters

TRUCAGE: Oh yes that! Well, let's see.. forgive me, my head is still spinning and... well, uh... the door, yes! (*to Ludos*) I say, do you remember..what was his name... Mr. Quincannon from the outing last year? Well as sure as I'm standing here, I thought it was him. And before you can say, Bob's your Uncle, I was grabbed in a restraining manner. A bag placed over my head.

(a few beats)

DARLA: And then?

TRUCAGE: And then?

NICK: Loud noises maybe? Kind of like... bang bang! Maybe gunshots?!

TRUCAGE: Right! Yes! I do recall some noises now that you mention it! As I said, a bag was placed over my head. I could not see. Perhaps there were.. yes! Of course, the gunshots. I imagine it was a diversionary tactic! I'm not quite sure why it was there. All I know is that I was bound up and left in what I believe to be the garden shed.

LUDOS: Oh deary me! Sounds like you have had quite a kerfuffle! Filled with assorted roughhousing! Here, have a seat poor fellow. You'll be right as rain in no time.

LUDOS leads TRUCAGE over to sit down.

TRUCAGE: It was frightening I tell you! It's getting so a fellow can't answer the door anymore!

Ludos, Trucage and Mendacio quietly stage talk upstage left as DARLA leads NICK downstage right to talk out of earshot of the three.

DARLA: OK! That's it! I'm done! Done with these people and this whole fruit loop gathering!

NICK: But Darla, we've (/) only...

DARLA: But Darla nothing! This is not normal. These people are not normal. This creepy place, not normal! This situation. These stories. These accents! Nothing that is going on here is...

NICK: Normal! Right. I think you've made your point and normally, I would say you're right. But there are too many loose ends.

DARLA: No loose ends Nick. No loose ends! Just some story about a bag and a garden shed. He wasn't shot. There's no dead body. He sitting over there just as sure as you please! The end is no longer loose!

NICK and DARLA silently converse as we now hear the other conversation

TRUCAGE: Sorry everyone for the worry!

MENDACIO: It's fine. Everything is.. fine now.

TRUCAGE: Good. Thank you Miss Mendacio. If it weren't for that peculiar business!

LUDOS: It's all peculiar business if you ask me. Those people are peculiar. This situation. These stories. Everything is peculiar.

TRUCAGE: Spot on I say! And strange having that nurse and the detective. It's a wonder they made it in this weather.

LUDOS: I wonder what they're talking about over there?

NICK and DARLA resume as the other three silently converse.

DARLA: I wonder what they're talking about over there?

NICK: Probably how fortunate they are that we arrived. You know, taking charge of the situation.

DARLA: Situation? What situation?

NICK: Well, the uh.... the....you know. Trucage thing.

DARLA: There was no Trucage thing. He was lost and now he is found.

NICK: And was blind but now... I see there's more going on here than meets the eye!

DARLA: And I don't like what I see! It's like we're in some bad B movie. You know the one with the amateur acting and the plot you've seen a million times. The car breaks down in the rain. The large estate. The Fellini characters. It's been done to death.

NICK: Possibly, but I'm still wondering about the subplot. If Trucage was grabbed when he answered the door and then bound up in a shed, why? And more to the point *Who?*

DARLA: Who cares? Let's go.

NICK: No, let's think about it, Darla! Let's use the little gray cells. Who knocked on the door? Who grabbed him and fired off shots? I can vouch for the ladies' whereabouts. We were upstairs and you were down here with Deidre and Trucage. That's everyone. And if that's everyone... then who did it? It seems we have an extra guest.

NICK and DARLA silently converse as we now hear the other conversation

LUDOS: If that's the case, then it seems we have extra guests.

MENDACIO: Should we arrange for extra refreshments?

LUDOS: Speaking of refreshments, I do wonder what's become of Miss Heinspiele?

TRUCAGE: I'm sure she's just fine.

NICK and DARLA resume as the other three silently converse.

DARLA: This is not a "who done it"! Nothing has been done to anyone.

DEIDRE enters

DEIDRE: Excuse me, I don't mean to interrupt but... I believe Miss Heinspiele is dead.

LUDOS: What?

TRUCAGE: Good Lord!

MENDACIO: Really?

DEIDRE: Yes.

NICK: *(to Darla)* What were you saying, dear?

LIGHTS DOWN

LIGHTS UP

CAPTAIN TRUCAGE is pacing. MRS LUDOS is seated on couch with MISS MEDACIO as the act opens. DEIDRE stands upstage.

LUDOS: Well, this turned out quite... interesting.

MENDACIO: But Miss Heinspiele?

TRUCAGE: It's the way the worm turns.

MENDACIO: But.. Miss Heinspiele?

LUDOS: I'm lead to believe it was poison in the ladyfingers. Perhaps meant for one of us.

TRUCAGE: Do you assume it was placed there, by one of us?

LUDOS: Or one of *them*.

TRUCAGE: You mean Shifty Sherlock and Nurse Ratchett? What are they doing out there anyway?

DEIDRE: Investigating I believe. Scouring for clues.

LUDOS: Deidre, If I'm not mistaken, you were out in the kitchen with Miss Heinspeile.

DEIDRE: Yes but...

MENDACIO: But Miss Heinspiele.

LUDOS: Why do you keep saying, *But Miss Heinspiele?*

MENDACIO: Because we were worried that Captain Trucage was ..

LUDOS: Was what? Captain Trucage is right here, isn't he? Quite alive?

TRUCAGE: Yes, yes he is. If I do say so myself. Close call at the door earlier. And as I said, I believe it was a diversion, to lure me away.

MENDACIO: Oh, I see! A diversion! A red salmon!

LUDOS: I believe you mean *red herring*.

TRUCAGE: Well, it's all fishy if you ask me. A person looking like Quincannon grabs and bounds me. Fires off a pistol and throws me in the shed! To what end?

MENDACIO: Well, I would think to Miss Heinspiele's end! It wasn't you in trouble Captain. But Miss Heinspiele! But maybe that's just me.

LUDOS: That *is just you* with all your nonsense utterances this evening.

MENDACIO: I will have you know Miss Ludos I do not utter nonsense!

LUDOS: It's all utter nonsense! I vote we bring this all to an end.

MENDACIO: You can't do that! We've just started!

LUDOS: Started? Nothing has gone to plan! Why go on?

NICK enters

NICK: Hello, excuse me?

LUDOS: Yes? Go on.

NICK: As you know, we have a bit of a situation here. Actually, a bit of a bummer situation. Bummer in the sense that.. we have what appears to be a homicide and to top it off, we have no way to contact the authorities.

TRUCAGE: Authorities? My dear man, we thought *you* were the authorities!

DEIDRE: I think it's the costume that's throwing you. It threw me.

NICK: Yes right, the costume. That was for some other deal. But right here, right now, my role will be as it is normally, and that's 'detective'. You can say 'investigation' is my calling. Speaking of calling, do any of you folks have a cell phone with a clear signal?

LUDOS: What on earth for?

NICK: What for? (*sighs*) For calling? You know, here on earth? (*taps his mouth a few times*) Is this thing on? Testing? One, Two!

TRUCAGE: Coming through loud and clear!

NICK: Good. I need a phone that works loud and clear because... Well, as I previously said we have a bit of thing here. A murdery type of deal.

TRUCAGE: I believe he means Miss Heinspiele. You know, the poison fingers,

NICK: Wait! What? No, no! There were no poisoned fingers. It's more like a strangled neck.

TRUCAGE: Strangled neck? (*To Ludos*) You said it was poison!

LUDOS: Did I? When did I say that?

TRUCAGE: A few moments ago. You said you were lead to believe it was poison on the ladyfingers. Possibly meant for one of us. But she was strangled! (*Gasps*) Do you think the strangled neck was meant for one of us?

NICK: Yea, OK. Anyway, If we could get back to the matter at hand... do any of you have..

DARLA enters quickly interrupting.

DARLA: Nick! Did you find a phone?

NICK: I was just working on that. We got a tad sidetracked.

TRUCAGE: Sorry old chap. Don't think my cell phone works here.

LUDOS: What about the house phone? Why don't you use it, if it's so important?

DARLA: We did try it. The line is dead.

MENDACIO: I have one. I believe I left it upstairs. I'll just go fetch it shall I?

LUDOS: If you must, then please, by all means! I'm sure the detective would appreciate it.

TRUCAGE: Are you sure it works here? It probably doesn't.

MENDACIO: Well, I don't know.. I mean...

NICK: I sure would appreciate that.

Miss Mendacio crosses and exits up right

DARLA: And I'm sure your friend Miss Heinspiele would appreciate the care and concern you all are expressing for her. I mean, is it me?

NICK: Being snarky? Yea, I think it is.

DARLA: I think it's a little disconcerting that a woman was strangled in the other room and you're all just sitting around playing Downton Abby!

DEIDRE: That's not what they're playing.

TRUCAGE: Well what are *you* playing at Detective person? What do you expect us to do? Yes, it is a tragedy about Miss Heinspiele and well all feel dreadful probably, but what can be done, I ask you?

NICK: Well, for starters we can try to figure out what happened! And by "happened" I mean, whose hands *happened* to go around Miss Heinspiele's neck.

LUDOS: Deidre was the last person to be with Miss Heinspiele.

DEIDRE: Yes, true. I was only with her for a moment. She asked for vanilla extract. I went to the pantry and when I returned she was... well, not needing the extract anymore.

NICK: How long were you away?

DEIDRE: Ten minutes at the most. I would have returned sooner but the light in the pantry was out. Fortunately, I knew where the candlesticks were.

NICK: Did you see or hear anything within those ten minutes?

DEIDRE: It was dark, I couldn't see anything. But I do believe I heard Miss Heinspiele say something. I thought I heard her say, "Oh, it's you."

TRUCAGE: Was it Quincannon? I thought it was when I said it.

LUDOS: Why didn't you say, "Oh it's you Quincannon!"?

DARLA: Victims never say the killer's name. Haven't you seen that movie?

TRUCAGE: Which movie?

DARLA: All of them.

NICK: Who is Quincannon anyway?

TRUCAGE: A gentleman from last year's event. Friendly chap. (*beat*) Or was.

LUDOS: He was a bit too friendly. He *was* not invited back after his behavior during the Red hour.

DARLA: What is this "red hour"?

TRUCAGE: It's just a mindless diversion to break up the evening. A chance to let our hair down and... I say! Do you think Quincannon could be behind this? Because he wasn't invited?

NICK: So he becomes a buzzkill tonight? Throws a sack over your head, fires a pistol, drags you off and then sneaks around back to strangle Heinspiele? Because he wasn't invited?

TRUCAGE: Could be.

NICK: It *could* imply that someone's lurking around. Someone that shouldn't be here.

LUDOS: It could be that he conducted his business and left. Why would he remain? I've heard of returning to the scene of the crime, but not remaining.

DARLA: Right! Who hangs around when they weren't invited? Right, Nick? Who would do that?

NICK: Right Darla. Who would do that? I can't imagine! In the meantime, I want to look around. Deidre, could you show me the pantry.

DEIDRE: Right this way. (*begins to exit*)

NICK: Everyone else, if you could just hang and chill.

LUDOS: Hang and chill?

DARLA: He means hang as in, No one may leave this home!

NICK: Right! What she said. The game is at hand! Or afoot! Or some body part to be determined.

NICK crosses and exits off with DEIDRE

END ACT ONE

ACT II

TRUCAGE, LUDOS are seated and DARLA paces

TRUCAGE: Well this is certainly playing out in an exciting way!

LUDOS: I don't know if I would call it exciting. I mean, do you honestly think someone would show up here and cause such a diversion?

DARLA: A diversion? A diversion from what?

TRUCAGE: These evenings have a usual pattern.

DARLA: They do?

TRUCAGE: Yes my dear girl

. Some of us enjoy a bit of skylarking if you will. Just a drop or two into the mix. A little jollification borrowed from our sword foam days. I mean, how would it be if we gathered and went about the same business, the same way? I wouldn't enjoy that.

MENDACIO enters with a cell phone

MENDACIO: Oh excuse me! I don't show any little thing-a-ma jiggles on my phone so I guess it's not working.

She shows Darla – Darla takes it to examine

DARLA: Well, you don't have it turned on for one thing.

MENDACIO: I don't? Silly me! I would have been down sooner but I couldn't find the short cut down through the kitchen.

DARLA: The short cut through the kitchen?

LUDOS: Yes. The back passage in the upper hallway that leads down to the kitchen. I believe it was the servant's staircase. All those that have *been* here before know about it.

MENDACIO: I knew about it and couldn't find it. I just split the difference and came down the front.

TRUCAGE: I'm not sure I knew about it. Did I?

LUDOS: Anyway, most of our guests know about it. The details of the estate are included in our guidelines. Which are included in the announcement on our invitations.

DARLA: Invitations? *(is looking intent at Mendacio's cell phone)*

MENDACIO: Yes. The invitations to our event here at Chipping Cleghorn. You should know that Nurse Christie! May I have my phone back now?

DARLA: Oh! Of course! *(gives cell back)* Right! *(thinking -crosses downstage away from group)* Chipping Cleghorn? Where do I know that name?

DEIDRE enters crossing to LUDOS, MENDACIO and TRUCAGE – They speak in a group as if out of earshot of DARLA

DEIDRE: *(to Ludos)* I think there's a bit of a problem here.

A MURDER HAS BEEN RENOUNCED

DARLA speaks facing down stage not realizing they are not listening as she speaks- nor are they paying attention to her

DARLA: I think there's a bit of a problem or misunderstanding here.

LUDOS: (*speaking to Deidre*) What is the problem?

DARLA: OK, see the deal is.. about these invitations.

DEIDRE: First of all, they (*indicates Darla*) are *not* invited guests to our event.

DARLA: We aren't one of your guests.

DEIDRE: They *are* stranded travelers. Not PC's in our venture.

DARLA: We were on our way to a costume party and came here hoping to use your phone.

DEIDRE: A real detective and a real nurse.

DARLA: We told Deidre when we arrived. I explained it but...

LUDOS: (*no accent*) That explains quite a bit.

DARLA: ...maybe I wasn't clear.

DEIDRE: It doesn't explain the fact that Trudy.. *is* dead. Literally. Not as a part of the free from. But in actuality.

TRUCAGE: Trudy? Good Lord! But how did.. ? I thought that...

LUDOS: You're kidding!

DEIDRE: I wish I was. See for yourselves.

TRUCAGE, MENDACIO and LUDOS quickly exit off left – NICK enters at same time

DARLA: I'm not sure what kind of gathering this is here tonight but, whoever you think I am, I'm not.

NICK: Who are you then?

DARLA: (*turning to see they've left*) What? Where did they go?

NICK: They all went into the kitchen.

DARLA: But I was talking to them!

NICK: I know I heard you.

DARLA: Nick listen, there's something weird going on here.

NICK: I've heard you say that before also.

DARLA: I think I've figured it out. Chipping Cleghorn! I know where I've heard that before. It's from a book! It's a fictional place in Agatha Christie stories.

NICK: How fitting. I mean, what with the murder and all.

DARLA: Don't you understand? The accents, the bizarre conversations! It's as if we stepped into some fictional world. Look at how calm they were when they learned their friend was strangled. Whatever is going on here, they think we're part of it! The detective and the nurse. We fit into it! But we aren't in it We're just here for a phone.

NICK: Right! Just a phone! Is that too much to ask?

DARLA: Mendacio went up to get her phone, acting as if she didn't have it all night! But I'm sure she been using it.

NICK: Using it? How do you know?

DARLA: She had texts from tonight. I only saw one that said "Juno or Tru-no.. Ink.. itches... or something.

NICK: Are you finished with your something because I have something too.

DARLA: What's your something?

A MURDER HAS BEEN RENOUNCED

NICK: (*searches pockets*) When I was in the kitchen with Deidre checking out the pantry I heard her say something. I thought she was speaking to me so I stepped out and saw her talking to Heinspiele. She bent down to check for a pulse and turned white as a ghost and said, '*This is real! Trudy is really dead.*'

DARLA: Really dead? As opposed to what? Dubiously dead?

NICK: Long story short, I assured her that, I was a real detective and our being here tonight was an accident-stance. She got it. Now hopefully they all get it. (*pulls out notebook*) Ah! Got it!

DARLA: I was trying to explain but they left and... wait! Won't they contaminate they crime scene?

NICK: I secured the body best I could. (*consults notebook*) I believe Heinspiele was strangled with something. There are ligature marks on her neck not much in the way of fingerprints. She was lying face down. And there was a little red towel placed on her back. Not sure what the deal is there.

DARLA: It's time we went to work and got the bottom of this nutty night.

NICK: Right. I need to check the grounds for footprints or any sign of someone else.

DARLA: There's a passage! They were telling me there's a servant's staircase that leads to the kitchen.

NICK: OK You check that out, I'll check outside. If I'm not back in 20 minutes, then... I probably needed more time, so add another 10 or 15.

They Exit - lights down

Lights up

LUDOS, TRUCAGE, MENDACIO and DEIDRE are standing around. Their demeanor is different –and they speak naturally – no accents

MENDACIO: Well, this is a problem! That means that we... What do we do now? Split the prize?

TRUCAGE: Maybe Melinda is right. Maybe we should call the evening done. In light of the circumstances. Who was the Game Master on this one?

DEIDRE: I am. Or was.

TRUCAGE: *(to Ludos)* I thought *you* were Emily.

LUDOS: No, I was Game Master last month when we did "Curse Of the Last Will".

TRUCAGE: Well this whole thing was a bust! Most of the people didn't show up because of the weather. It's hard playing this out with only a few of us.

LUDOS: Yes and there were a *few* weren't a part of it.

TRUCAGE: But I admit, they fit in nicely. Especially that nurse. Hot-see Tot-see!

LUDOS: Edwin! It is exactly that kind of thing that got Quincannon banned from our events.

MENDACIO: Do we think it was him? He came back and strangled Trudy?

DEIDRE: What would he have against Trudy?

TRUCAGE: Maybe he was being inappropriate. He got a little too, you know, hands-on and she spurned his advances and he didn't take it very well.

LUDOS: What's hard form me to take is this business about him grabbing you at the door and shooting a gun.

TRUCAGE: Why would I make up something like that?

LUDOS: How do we know this detective isn't made up? Did anyone see a badge?

DEIDRE: I have no reason to doubt him. He may have reason to doubt us. What must he think of us? Here we are, playing our (/) game and...

TRUCAGE: We thought they were part of it! Probably thought we were a bunch of loonies.

DEIDRE: We should probably explain. (*exits*)

TRUCAGE: Very well. Shall we find them and...?

MENDACIO: I don't know about you but I could use some coffee first

TRUCAGE: Yes! As could I. I would even split the last Danish with someone.

MENDACIO: I'll split it with you.

TRUCAGE: Fine. We can.. talk about.. things.

MENDACIO, TRUCAGE and LUDOS exits left. After a few beats DARLA enters right, She is holding some papers (legal size) reading them over. She is reading silently and then begins reading out loud

DARLA: Player characters? Heinspiele, Trudy Osbourne? Captain Trucage.. Edwin Murphy? Melinda Stahlhaus..? (*continues reading*) Rules and boundaries shall be as follows... death will be determined by a red flag... clues will be set on an hour before...

DARLA crosses quickly right as if to run out toward front door, just as she does NICK enters they almost collide.

NICK: Darla! Funny running into you here!

DARLA: NICK! Stop doing that! (*smacks him with papers*) Here! Look at this. I found it upstairs. (*hands him papers*)

NICK: What's this? More dirt on the crazed killer? (*begins reading*)

DARLA: In a manner of speaking. That explains pretty much everything! Read it!

NICK: I'm trying! (*takes a few beats to read*) It's instructions of some sort. And.. rules of (/) some game.

DARLA: None of this is real! It's all fake. The newspaper. The killer! It's a game. A larp!

NICK: A lark?

DARLA: No Larp! A game! It's all been a game! The winner stands to receive 10,000 dollars!

NICK: What 'chu talkin bout Willis?

LUDOS enters from left

LUDOS: I thought I heard someone.

Darla takes paper from Nick and consults it.

DARLA: Yes! Here we are. Nick, may I introduce Emily Brent!

NICK: Brent? I thought her name was Ludos.

DARLA: Emily has been assuming the role of Miss Ludos this evening. It's her PC or Player character in the game.

Trucage enters.

NICK: Her player character?

DARLA: And this is Edwin Murphy who has been identifying as Captain Montgomery Trucage

NICK: Has he? OK. Hi. How's it goin?

TRUCAGE: (EDWIN): Pretty well. Yourself?

NICK: Not bad. Can't complain.

TRUCAGE: (To Ludos) So, the truth is out.

LUDOS (EMILY): Yes, it's reared it's ugly head.

DEIDRE enters

DARLA: And this should be Vera Claythorne.

NICK: And Jerry Mathers as the beaver.

DEIDRE (VERA): I'm assuming they know now?

NICK: Yes, we know now! *(turns to Darla)* OK Help me out here Darla. What do we know?

DARLA: *(reading) A Mystery Night At Cleghorn.* An evening of murder and thievery! A role-playing game for up to 10 guests or more.

NICK: Game? These people have playing... this has all been...?

LUDOS (EMILY): You must forgive us.

DARLA: One big LARP.

NICK: Of course it is! Naturally. Any fool could see that it's... *(Beat)* What is it?

DEIDRE (VERA): *Live Action Role Play* or "LARP". Imagine the board game of Clue but on a larger scale. Played out live, in real-time with real people. We all assume roles in the game and act it out.

NICK: You mean like D and D? *(begins digging in pockets for notepad)*

DEIDRE (VERA): But without the dragons, dungeons, and swords.

DARLA: That explains the accents and strange behavior!

DEIDRE (VERA): We each assume a character that has a list of goals. Edwin was Captain Trucage. A petty thief with questionable intentions. Emily was Miss Ludos, the stock matron and I was Deidre the sarcastic domestic of the estate.

DARLA: So, whose estate is this?

DEIDRE (VERA): It belongs to Emily. She is kind enough to allow us to use her home.

LUDOS (EMILY): It's very fitting for our games. Which of course we make up as we go. That's what makes it fun! We get together a few times a year and have this event. It livens up this dreary old place.

TRUCAGE: (EDWIN): You never can tell what will happen. Heck, half the time we don't know who will turn up and be a part of it.

DEIDRE (VERA): Hence the confusion with you. This particular game included stranded travelers.

LUDOS (EMILY): A nurse and a detective. But apparently, the weather prevented everyone from being here.

DARLA: Except for us. The real stranded travelers. The real detective and nurse.

NICK: And we have a real murder. What are the odds? One co-winky dink after another!

DARLA: So was Heinspiele or Trudy supposed to be the victim tonight?

DEIDRE (VERA): Anyone can be the victim, it's not set in stone. Anything can happen. I was the Game master tonight, which means I am in charge and oversee all elements of the story we create. I verify game casualties.

DARLA: How do you verify? How do you know someone is dead in the game?

DEIDRE (VERA): A red flag or tea towel is placed on the victim. Since anyone of us could be the killer, we all carry one. To.. you know, remove someone from the game.

MENDACIO enters from left

MENDACIO: Oh! I didn't know where everyone went! I thought we were going up the back stairs.

LUDOS (EMILY): I believe you all know Melinda Stahlhaus.

MENDACIO (MELINDA): *(still using an accent)* Delighted to make your acquaintance!

LUDOS (EMILY): You can cut it Mel. We're off game.

NICK: *(still searching pockets)* So let me paste this Jackson Pollack together into a clearer picture. This evening was *pretend*. A game. A simulated mystery. *A make-believe* victim and a *make-believe* killer. *(finds notepad -now searches for pencil)*

DEIDRE (VERA): Correct. And the goal of the game would be one or more of us figuring out who the killer is.

DARLA: Who *was* the killer in this game?

DEIDRE (VERA): It could be anyone. It just plays out as we go.

NICK: But *this* game played out with a deadly role of the die. Heinspiele wasn't a role play victim but a real-time victim. So it goes without saying... but I will, there is a real-time killer.

TRUCAGE: (EDWIN): Someone in this very room!

MENDACIO (MELINDA): Or someone *outside* this room.

NICK: Speaking of which, I did check outside. *(consults notes)* Fortunately, our torrential downpour is now just a trivial dampening. I did find a set of footprints, which I believe were yours.. Captain...uh..

TRUCAGE: (EDWIN): Edwin. Or Eddy is fine.

NICK: OK Captain Eddie. I also found what I believe to be a second set of prints. Let me ask you, this person who grabbed you, was he a heavyset guy, medium or smallish?

TRUCAGE: (EDWIN): Well, I would say.. the person was by no means smallish. They overpowered me!

NICK: I also found some footprints around the back leading to the kitchen door. Which would appear to be a different size and then the Captains.

LUDOS (EMILY): (*gasps*) So this person came in the back into the kitchen and killed Trudy?

NICK: Maybe. Maybe not. They left tracks up to the door but no tracks on the kitchen floor. Perhaps they took off their shoes. Or maybe they came down the back stairs. Or were hiding in the kitchen.

MENDACIO (MELINDA): Maybe in the pantry!

NICK: Deidre was in the food pantry at the time. he only thing hiding in there is way expired cans of creamed corn.

LUDOS (EMILY): I thought you said the light was out. How did you see anything?

NICK: I always carry a light-emitting diode. (*shows a small flashlight*) Standard issue for a detective. I found the light bulb had been broken. Funny that huh? While exploring outside I saw that the phone line had been tampered with. Bulbs broke, lines fiddled with, all very classic in cases like this. Was this part of your game?

TRUCAGE: (EDWIN): That would have been good! But no. Not part of our game. I don't think.

DARLA: Part of someone's game. If Trudy were the intended target, I have to wonder, how would they know she would be going into the kitchen?

MENDACIO (MELINDA): That's true! Anyone might have gone out there. It could have been me.

LUDOS (EMILY): Or me. I did go out to the kitchen to tell Trudy the red hour was starting.

MENDACIO (MELINDA): And I went out to flip the circuit breaker! I was there in the dark! It's a wonder I made it out alive!

LUDOS (EMILY): But what about the footprints leading to the back door! It implies they came in through the back door.

MENDACIO (MELINDA): Or came in the back door and went up the back stairs. Or down the back stairs and out the door. Or maybe (/) they went...

LUDOS (EMILY): Thank you, Melinda. We get the picture.

NICK: Let's look at the *big* picture with a little paint by numbers if you will. The first color will be motive. So, who had it in for Heinspiele.

LUDOS (EMILY): Her real name was Trudy. She was a sweetheart. Not an evil bone in her body. I can't think of anyone who *had it in* for her.

TRUCAGE: (EDWIN): I had nothing against her. I've done many of these events with her. A great player! How about you Vera?

DEIDRE (VERA): No. I only knew her from the games here. Not socially outside of there.

TRUCAGE: (EDWIN): Melinda?

MENDACIO (MELINDA): Me? Not in a million years! I can't think of anyone here who would want to strangle Trudy.

NICK: OK our next color is opportunity. Let's paint some happy little bushes with that. When our victim went out into the kitchen, the rest of you were.... ?

LUDOS (EMILY): I was right here. And so was Vera and Melinda.

MENDACIO (MELINDA): That's right! It was time for the red hour. We were all right here. But.. (*To Ludos*) Emily, you did go out there to tell her the red hour was starting.

LUDOS (EMILY): Well yes, but I was only there for a moment. Not long enough to... do anything.

NICK: (to Mendacio) And you went out to flip the circuit breaker?

MENDACIO (MELINDA): Well, yes. I.. I did. But it was dark as you know. I followed the wall with my hand. I called out to Trudy. I said, "Hi Trudy, it's me, Melinda. I'm trying to find the circuit breaker." And she said. "Let me." Or something.

DARLA: Did you hear her say, *Oh it's you* or someone stumbling?

MENDACIO (MELINDA): The stumbling was me. I almost fell in front of the sink. I think there was something on the floor.

NICK: When the lights came back on where was Trudy? Where was she standing?

MENDACIO (MELINDA): She was at the fuse box. And she was very much alive at that time! Standing there. I mean, otherwise, I doubt she could have flipped the switch.

NICK: Where do we stand? We have a portrait of motive and opportunities, now we need to frame it. I would like each of you to explore this place. Look for anything out of place or any clues. Imagine you're playing your game.

MENDACIO (MELINDA): And what are we looking for?

LUDOS (EMILY): Clues Melinda. And anyone hiding.

NICK: Yes. Brilliant. Look for anyone or anything that doesn't belong. Minus of course, Darla and me.

TRUCAGE: (EDWIN): Great idea! Ladies if you want me to take the lead. You know, just in case!

LUDOS (EMILY): Very good Edwin. Lead away!

TRUCAGE: (EDWIN) exits off right followed by LUDOS (EMILY), DEIDRE (VERA) and MENDACIO (MELINDA) - NICK and DARLA remain.

DARLA: So what are we going to do?

NICK: Wait and see what they do. If anyone of them is guilty, this is the part where they make a mistake.

DARLA: But what about this mysterious Quincannon guy?

NICK: There were some extra footprints outside.

DARLA: Do you think he would sneak in through the back door and strangled Trudy?

NICK: Could be. And he could be part of the game

DARLA: What do you mean, part of the game?

NICK: Well if it's like they said, free form, and they just make it up as they go, maybe someone is making up quite a few extra bits and bobs tonight.

DARLA: How do we know what is real and what's the game? How do we tell?

NICK: Become a player!

DARLA: That's stupid Nick!

NICK: The saying is, don't hate the player, hate the game! So let's go outside and play bit of hide and seek.

DARLA: But it's muddy. I don't want to get my shoes dirty. They cost a (/) lot of..

NICK: I think you may be onto something dear Darla! The game really is *afoot or maybe a shoe*. Follow me! This I what I want you to do....

NICK speaks silently to DARLA as they exit off left

Lights down

Lights up

TRUCAGE: (EDWIN) enters from right followed by MENDACIO (MELINDA) and DEIDRE (VERA)

MENDACIO (MELINDA): Well, I didn't find anything or anyone.

TRUCAGE: (EDWIN): Nope. Me either.

DEIDRE (VERA): Do we know what happened to the necklace?

MENDACIO (MELINDA): Necklace? What necklace?

DEIDRE (VERA): From the game. That one was taken.

TRUCAGE: (EDWIN): Oh that! Right. I know where that is. (looks around)

EDWIN goes to couch and lifts cushion. He feels around. Lifts another searching.

TRUCAGE: (EDWIN): (*cont.*) It was right here! I swear I stuck it in here.

MENDACIO (MELINDA): Maybe someone took it!

TRUCAGE: (EDWIN): Yes. *Me!* I took it. I'm the petty thief character.

DEIDRE (VERA): I think she means someone *else*. As in stole it *from* you.

TRUCAGE: (EDWIN): Who would steal something I already stole?! That makes no sense!

DEIDRE (VERA): It makes no sense killing Trudy either.

TRUCAGE: (EDWIN): No. No it doesn't. Why I should worry about a silly necklace? (*beat*) I guess now, with Trudy being... you know, that we.... I mean, I guess that eliminates the overall prize. What are the rules about this Vera? I can't remember.

DEIDRE (VERA): When there's no winner, there's a split between players.

TRUCAGE: (EDWIN): So, it would be five ways then? Or four I guess.

DEIDRE (VERA): I was the Game Master so technically, I'm out. It would be three ways.

MENDACIO (MELINDA): But you should get something Vera. It almost doesn't seem right to do.

LUDOS (EMILY) enters from right.

LUDOS (EMILY): What doesn't seem right?

TRUCAGE (EDWIN): Everything about this night. Did you find anything?

LUDOS (EMILY): No I didn't. The only thing I found is this to be the worst event ever!

DEIDRE (VERA): I know Emily. I feel awful about what happened. Maybe the detective has found something.

TRUCAGE: (EDWIN): I doubt it.

NICK enters from left.

NICK: Hello peeps, how's it going? Anything to report? *(takes out small notebook)*

TRUCAGE: (EDWIN): Nothing on my end. I searched this place top to bottom.

NICK makes notes throughout following exchanges

NICK: That would include all of your personal belongings? Your clothes or do you come dressed in costume all ready?

DEIDRE (VERA): Yes. We come dressed for the occasion.

NICK: Shoes as well?

DEIDRE (VERA): Yes. The idea of the game to enter in character and leave in character.

NICK: And as these characters, you make it up as you go and whatever happens, *happens* right?

DEIDRE (VERA): Well yes, for the most part. But we have guidelines, a theme..

LUDOS (EMILY): For instance, this particular game had an Agatha Christie theme. A Murder Has Been Announced or Ten Little Indians, something along those lines.

NICK: And within those lines, how do you win this game?

DEIDRE (VERA): Well, the players guess the murderer. If they think they know, they write it down and place it in the "Guess" jar. Whoever is the first to guess correctly, wins.

NICK: A guess jar? We have a swear jar at my house. Anyway, who monitors this Guess Jar?

DEIDRE (VERA): That would be me. I check the jar frequently and make notes.

NICK: And when you guess correctly and become the winner, you get the big prize money.

LUDOS (EMILY): Yes. Ten thousand dollars.

NICK: And where does this money come from?

DEIDRE (VERA): Entry fees. Each player pays around thousand to play.

LUDOS (EMILY): We were expecting ten guests this evening but...

NICK: But what if no one wins. No one guesses correctly?

DEIDRE (VERA): The victim gets the money.

NICK: Hmmm. Interesting. I'm sure it's probably in your rules. Darla was showing me the... Speaking of which, where did my wife get to? Darla? Oh Darla?

Darla enters from right.

DARLA: Yes! I'm here. I was finishing up... doing the.. you know... thing.

NICK: And a thing a wise man once said, "Eliminate the impossible, and whatever remains, however improbable must be the truth" . The truth here is that you all have *remained*. I would like to continue *the game*. And what I mean, is I would like you all to cast your vote. To use your guess jar.

DARLA: Yes. Play along. Just as you would have in your *Mystery Night At Cleghorn*.

MENDACIO (MELINDA): But so many strange things have happened outside of the normal game. And besides, I thought that this Quincannon man was (/) the...

TRUCAGE: (EDWIN): Yes! Melinda has a valid point! The game is off the rails. I say until this Quincannon business is sorted out, that we (/)can't really..

NICK: I want you to take old Quinty out of the running. Out of the picture. Forget him. Only vote for the people in this room.

LUDOS (EMILY): But in our game we have clues! And a clear idea of some sort!

DARLA: Just consider the facts. Several people went out into the kitchen when Trudy was there. Oh sure, they said they spoke with her and everything was fine but..how do you know? How much do you trust each other? That's what we would like to find out by your votes.

TRUCAGE: (EDWIN): You want us to do this.. now?

MENDACIO (MELINDA): Where's the guess jar?

DEIDRE (VERA): I believe it 's upstairs.

LUDOS (EMILY): Very well! Let's get to it.

They all exit off Right – ad-libbing with each other. At this point, the audience can be invited to Vote. NICK and DARLA can break the 4th wall and handle instructions or if you wish to keep the 4 walls closed – someone else can. The cast can help collect votes.

LUDOS (EMILY) , TRUCAGE: (EDWIN), DEIDRE (VERA) and MENDACIO (MELINDA) all gather on stage – sitting etc..

NICK and DARLA enter – Darla carries jar with (cast) votes. Nick searches for and finds his notepad.

NICK: Welcome back my friends to the show that never ends! My lovely assistant Darla has your votes and as to who the winner is... well, it's anybody's guess.

MENDACIO (MELINDA): What about your guess? You're the detective.

NICK: Yes. Yes I am. I spent 15 years on the force before going into private work. I can still detect facts. But enough about me. Who is our first contestant tonight Darla?

DARLA: *(taking paper slip from jar)* Our first contestant is.... *(reads)* Emily Brent!

NICK: Emily Brent! Come on down!

LUDOS (EMILY): What? I don't understand why I even have a vote! I wasn't in the kitchen with Trudy.

NICK: You are correct Emily!. Although you stated you went out to let Trudy know that the Red hour was about to begin, I think it's not very likely you're the evildoer. Our next contestant!

DARLA: *(taking paper slip from jar)* Our next contestant is... *(reads)* Vera Claythorne.

LUDOS (EMILY): Right! Vera was the GM, so technically not eligible.

MENDACIO (MELINDA): She was in the kitchen with Trudy!

NICK: Yes she was. However, Vera was the one who discovered Trudy's true fate. Why would a killer announce to everyone their victim's demise?

MENDACIO (MELINDA): Well, to throw suspicion away from themselves.

NICK: That only happens in the movies, right Darla?

DARLA: In about twenty that I can think of. Cut back to you Nick.

NICK: Fade in on our next vote.

DARLA: *(taking paper slip from jar)* And we zoom in on.. .*(reads)* Vera Claythorne again!

NICK: What do you guys have against poor Vera?

TRUCAGE: (EDWIN): As Melinda said, she was the only one with opportunity. I was accosted at (/) the door and....

LUDOS (EMILY): Please Ed! We've heard the story too many times now.

NICK: She's right! Too many stories we have all heard before. My wife pointed that out to me earlier tonight. This night is riddled with cliches. Let me present one more cliché, follow the money and you'll find your culprit.

TRUCAGE: (EDWIN): Money? What money? There's no money. No one won! The game is over.

DARLA: Is it? As I understand the rules, you all will now split the prize four ways.

TRUCAGE: (EDWIN): Three ways.

NICK: Which ain't bad for a night's work. I think some of you had your heart set on splitting it 2 ways. Which ain't bad to boot. Or should I say shoe! *(beat)* That's your first cue, Darla.

DARLA: Right! Sorry. (*she hurries off left exits*)

LUDOS (EMILY): What is this about?

NICK: This is about game theory, or my theories about your game. (*consults notepad*) As I understand this, when the murder happens in your game, you place a red flag on the victim. And you each carry one because *anyone* could be the killer. One was used on Trudy. So, may I see your cloths?

Everyone except DEIDRE (VERA) pulls out their red cloth.

DEIDRE (VERA): I do not carry one because I was the game master.

TRUCAGE: (EDWIN): And we all have ours!

A MURDER HAS BEEN RENOUNCED

NICK: Trudy was a player correct? Therefore she would've had a red cloth of her own. We could assume, her own cloth was placed on her.

TRUCAGE: (EDWIN): Oh. Right. Of course. That makes sense.

NICK: What doesn't make sense is, the cloth on Trudy was rather damp. I realize she was in the kitchen and kitchens are places where dampness can be a thing, but we can't ignore the fact that dampness has also been a thing outside tonight. So we have a missing necklace and damp cloth. What does that add up to?

MENDACIO (MELINDA): Maybe someone dropped their red cloth...in the sink?

LUDOS (EMILY): Or maybe it came from outside.

TRUCAGE: (EDWIN): Maybe we should wait till the authorities get here and sort it all out.

NICK: And maybe someone here will have more time to cover their tracks. Trust me. It all adds up. Melinda, may I borrow your phone for a minute, I want to use your calculator?

MENDACIO (MELINDA): *(reluctantly)* Ummm.. sure I guess. *(hands it to him)*

NICK: Thank you. Let's see, *(going through phone)* The square root of murder, times pie... carry the one. Ah ha!

TRUCAGE: (EDWIN): What are you doing?

DARLA enters holding a pair of men's shoes.

DARLA: Got 'em!

LUDOS (EMILY): Whose are those?

DARLA: They belong to our elusive Mr. Quincannon!

MENDACIO (MELINDA): So he *was* here!

DARLA: Only in spirit. You see, Nick and I believe the role of Mr. Quincannon was played by someone else here.

NICK: Why you ask? Go ahead ask.

MENDACIO (MELINDA): OK. Why?

NICK: Good question! If you can make it up as you go and anything can happen, why couldn't someone make up their own little game inside the big game? A little game of I'll let you murder me and then I create a diversion so crazy it ll throw everyone off. No one will guess the killer. And if no one guesses correctly, per the rules, the victim gets the grand prize. And then the victim splits it with the killer.

LUDOS (EMILY): OK but how would you throw everyone off?

NICK: Easy. Just like it was accomplished tonight. Introduce the potential for a mystery guest. One who comes and knocks on the door. Fires some blanks so that gunshots are heard. Leave footprints for us to find that don't match anyone here. No body is found. The game is a draw. And the prize is split between the conspirators.

DARLA: And this is usually the part where the guilty party panics and stands up (/) and

TRUCAGE: (EDWIN): (*stands*) All right! Hold the phone! Are you suggesting that I made up the whole thing to throw everyone off by pretending to be shot and then hid in the shed so they couldn't find me!

NICK: Yes Captain Eddie, pretty much! Spot on old boy! We are also suggesting that you had an accomplice. Who placed men's shoes on. Snuck out the back, came around to the front, (/) where...

DARLA: Where she knocked at the front door. If you recall, I was here at the time when you went to answer. Shots were fired so that I would hear, concluding you had been the victim in the game. And you disappeared so the rules of the game could be tested!

TRUCAGE: (EDWIN): What? That's nonsense!

NICK: I found the pistol loaded with blanks out behind the shed.

DARLA: And I found these shoes and this under the sink. Shoes your accomplice used.

NICK: The funny part of the story is I think you did something foolish. Something wacky. Dare I say careless. I think you became bored waiting out there and tried to sneak around to the kitchen. Perhaps feeling parched or peckish. Whatever the case, while you were there Trudy came out and almost saw you.

DARLA: You ducked into the pantry. Breaking the light bulb so you couldn't be seen. While there you sent a desperate text message to your accomplice.

NICK: In your panic, you left the shoes by the sink. Along with your red cloth.

DARLA: And this! (*holds up necklace*)

TRUCAGE: (EDWIN): But I put that under the cushions in the couch!

NICK: I'm sure you did. But you or your accomplice retrieved it again. And you made sure others were around as you went to retrieve it, making it seem that someone had taken it. Again throwing everyone off your trail.

TRUCAGE: (EDWIN): What are you implying detective? If you're trying to say that I or someone strangled Trudy with that necklace?

DEIDRE (VERA): He didn't imply that.

LUDOS (EMILY): No Edwin. He didn't. *You* did.

TRUCAGE: (EDWIN): I did? Well, darn it! But.. but... where's your proof?!

NICK: Right here on Melinda's phone. These text messages.

MENDACIO (MELINDA): (*tries to grab phone*) Oh that! That's nothing.

NICK: (*reading from Melinda phone*) Tru-nose.. In kitch... .. left red flag shoe in kitch plea get! Will creet diversion front. Around neck and Kill her. Which I believe translates very roughly into *Trudy knows. She's in the kitchen, left red flag and shoes. Please get. I will create a diversion around the front. Get Necklace. And Kill her.*

TRUCAGE: (EDWIN): It was supposed to say "Tell Her"! Not *kill* her! Bloody auto-correct!

MENDACIO (MELINDA): I didn't know!

TRUCAGE: (EDWIN): Why would I say *kill her*? Stupid woman! We could have had a 3 way split with Trudy. You just had to tell her! She would've been in on it!

MENDACIO (MELINDA): You said *around neck*!

TRUCAGE: (EDWIN): I meant the necklace! I'll go around front! Get the necklace! It was dark I could see the buttons clearly!

DEIDRE (VERA): Wait! You were going to trick us and split the prize!

LUDOS (EMILY): Do you mean to tell me that you two killed Trudy!

TRUCAGE: (EDWIN): I didn't! *She* did!

MENDACIO (MELINDA): It's not my fault you can't spell! Also not my fault you left the stupid red flag on the sink! And the shoes! I fell over them!

TRUCAGE: (EDWIN): And it's not my fault you can't delete your messages!

MENDACIO (MELINDA): I didn't have time! I was lucky I could get out in the kitchen to clean up your mess!

DARLA: Trudy saw what you left in the sink. Perhaps she even saw you lurking in the kitchen. It wouldn't take long for her to figure it out. To figure out the scenario you had come up with. She would tell Vera and you little cheating plan would have failed

DEIDRE (VERA): And you would have been disqualified.

TRUCAGE: (EDWIN): Not if Melinda would have told her!

LUDOS: (EMILY): She never would have been a part of it!

TRUCAGE (EDWIN): We'll never know now, will we Melinda?

DEIDRE (VERA): (to Edwin) But why did you come back in? With that Quincannon story about being tied up? What was that all about?

NICK: A little more free form improvising on his part. You see his first plan hit a major snag. He needed a way to cover his tracks. Probably found some rope and a gag and came up with the kidnap story.

DARLA: What else could he do but try to salvage the game by reappearing and trying to cover up his cheats. He made up his crazy Quincannon story to cover the footprints he had Melinda plant. He had to explain them now. He knew we would find them. Introduce a new story for the evening. With Trudy on board, perhaps the creepy Quincannon could reappear and claim a new victim. He could place his red flag on her in the kitchen.

You all would have been so confused no one could guess the killer.

TRUCAGE: (EDWIN): It would have worked too!

DARLA: Right if hadn't been for those meddling kids!

NICK: That and a deadly typo.

TRUCAGE: (EDWIN): I swear I put "Tell her!" not "Kill her!" So technically, I'm innocent.

NICK: I'm sure a judge and jury will have fun with that one. (*dials out on Mel's phone*)

LUDOS (EMILY): In all my years of these events, this has to be the craziest game scenario. Did you think you'd get away with it?

DARLA: They almost did. If they would have found a better disposal method for the shoes, the gun and the necklace. We might have never tied it all together.

TRUCAGE: (EDWIN): (*To Melinda*) Why did you throw them under the sink?!

MENDACIO (MELINDA): Why did you throw the gun behind the shed?

TRUCAGE: (EDWIN): You had plenty of time to (/) get rid..

MENDACIO (MELINDA): No I didn't! Vera was out there in the pantry!

TRUCAGE: (EDWIN): You could have left the lights out longer!

MENDACIO (MELINDA): She turned them on! And you could have talked to her yourself, instead of running away like an idiot!

TRUCAGE: (EDWIN): Oh! I'm the idiot? I'm the idiot?

NICK: *(into phone)* Yes hello? This is private detective Nick Dashell. Hey, how's it going? *(Continues talking silently)*

MENDACIO (MELINDA): Why did you have to sneak in the kitchen? Why didn't you stay put?

DARLA: OK! Guys! Why don't we play a new game? It's called the quiet game or the right to remain silent. Melinda and Edwin you start!

DEIDRE (VERA): I don't know what we would have done, if you two hadn't shown up.

DARLA: Who knows? I'm sure even if our car didn't break down and we didn't wander in here, one of you would have spoiled their game.

DEIDRE (VERA): I would like to believe so. I wasn't buying that whole Quincannon story anyway. Some oddball from last year showing up here.

There is a knock at the door.

DARLA: Nick?! Nick! There's someone at the door!

NICK: *(covers phone)* What?

DARLA: The door! Someone knocking!

NICK: Well I'm not getting it this time! You get it, Darla.

DARLA: Nick!

TRUCAGE: (EDWIN): That's OK! I'll get it!

He runs off quickly and MENDACIO (MELINDA): follows as if to escape.

DARLA: They're getting away! Nick! Nick!

NICK: Chill Darla. It's just the local PD. Someone in the area heard the gunshots earlier and called. That will be them checking on us. Every thing's cool. I'm arranging a tow truck now. Then we can get a ride and still have enough time to make the costume party!

DARLA: Wonderful. And this is the part where the female protagonist sighs with her arms crossed. And the camera zooms in on her face as she rolls her eyes.

Lights out

The End

AFTERWORD

Before You Go

If you would please rate and review this book. As an independent writer, your reviews and ratings help to increase the discovery of my works online.

Thank you!

Lee Mueller

ALSO BY LEE MUELLER

Murder Me Always

Talk About A Murder

Death Of A Doornail

I'm Getting Murdered In The Morning

Remains To Be Seen

To Wake The Dead

An Irritation To A Murder

Last Call At Chez Mort

Death Near Dead Mans Holler

An Audition For A Murder

Basic On Stage Survival Guide For Amateur Actors

Short Stories

Idle Essence Tales Of Marvin

Street Ends No Outlet -Tales Of Marvin Also

Other

A Series Of Short Serious Plays

Printed in Great Britain
by Amazon